PROOF PASSIONATE

"You won't make it," Skye Fargo told the girl, Trudy Keyser. "You won't learn to survive in the wilderness. You're not grown-up enough."

"Damn you Fargo. I'm grown-up, a hell of a lot more than you know," she flung back.

"Guess I just haven't seen any signs of it," he said.

She strode toward him, anger in her face. Her mouth sought his and pressed hard, her tongue pushing out angrily, deeply.

"I'll show you signs," she muttered as she drew back, her fingers yanking buttons open. Her shirt fell away, and her breasts spilled out with their own eagerness.

Skye Fargo was a fair man. He was more than willing to let Trudy Keyser prove how grown-up she could be. . . .

THE TRAILSMAN
55

THIEF RIVER
SHOWDOWN

by

Jon Sharpe

A SIGNET BOOK

NEW AMERICAN LIBRARY

PUBLISHER'S NOTE

This novel is a work of fiction. Names, characters, places, and incidents either are the product of the author's imagination or are used fictitiously, and any resemblance to actual persons, living or dead, events, or locales is entirely coincidental.

NAL BOOKS ARE AVAILABLE AT QUANTITY DISCOUNTS
WHEN USED TO PROMOTE PRODUCTS OR SERVICES.
FOR INFORMATION PLEASE WRITE TO PREMIUM MARKETING DIVISION,
NEW AMERICAN LIBRARY, 1633 BROADWAY,
NEW YORK, NEW YORK 10019.

The first chapter of this book previously appeared in *Killer Clan*, the fifty-fourth volume in this series.

SIGNET TRADEMARK REG. U.S. PAT. OFF. AND FOREIGN COUNTRIES
REGISTERED TRADEMARK—MARCA REGISTRADA
HECHO EN CHICAGO, U.S.A.

SIGNET, SIGNET CLASSIC, MENTOR, PLUME, MERIDIAN AND NAL BOOKS
are published by New American Library,
1633 Broadway, New York, New York 10019

First Printing, July, 1986

1 2 3 4 5 6 7 8 9

PRINTED IN THE UNITED STATES OF AMERICA

The Trailsman

Beginnings . . . they bend the tree and they mark the man. Skye Fargo was born when he was eighteen. Terror was his midwife, vengeance his first cry. Killing spawned Skye Fargo, ruthless, cold-blooded murder. Out of the acrid smoke of gunpowder still hanging in the air, he rose, cried out a promise never forgotten.

The Trailsman, they began to call him, all across the West: searcher, scout, hunter, the man who could see where others only looked, his skills for hire but not his soul, the man who lived each day to the fullest, yet trailed each tomorrow. Skye Fargo, the Trailsman, the seeker who could take the wildness of a land and the wanting of a woman and make them his own.

Northwest Minnesota, 1860,
land of the north lakes and the
north winds, just below the Thief River . . .

1

He didn't expect to see a girl there. She spelled trouble, and she had no business being in that saloon.

There were saloons and there were saloons, and then there were upholstered sewers. The Bent Wheel Saloon was an upholstered sewer—filthy, dark, with one long bar and a dozen battered tables, torn drapes and peeling paint. It was a place filled with pack rats, bums and boozers—men on the run, some from the world, some from themselves. The girl was as out of place as a spring gentian in a swamp.

She was pretty in a pert, pugnacious way, a round-cheeked face, a little snub nose with a row of freckles on it, short brown hair. She wore a shirt of dark-green checks over Levi's, a Walker sticking from the waist-band of her outfit. Not tall, she had a firm, young shape, a round little rear, and very high, almost conelike breasts.

She was in trouble now, and he watched the trio of men that had half-surrounded her. The ringleader, a tall, thin figure, pasty-faced with a wispy excuse of a beard, grinned obscenely as he moved toward her.

"You come in here, girlie, you got to give us a little feel," he said, and his hand stretched out to touch her breasts.

She knocked his hand away and held her ground. "Don't you touch me, you piece of slime," she snapped.

"Now, that's no way for you to talk, girlie. You're gonna get old Nick mad at you," the man said.

"I'll put a bullet in old Nick's gut," the girl said.

Fargo shook his head with grudging admiration. She was a tough little character. Tough but foolish. From where he sat in a corner of the saloon he saw one of the other two men circle around to come up behind her. She was completely unaware of him, all her attention on the pasty-faced man in front of her. As Fargo watched, the figure behind her sprang and pinned her arms to her side. A stocky man with a flat, broad face, he laughed harshly as he held the girl. The one who'd called himself Nick snapped his hand out, yanked the gun from the girl's waist, and sent it skittering across the floor.

"You won't be needing that, girlie." He laughed as he pressed both hands to her breasts, rubbing them back and forth as the stocky man held her. Fargo saw the girl's foot come up and lash out in a short, high kick.

"Ow," the one called Nick screamed, and clapped both hands to his groin as he sank to his knees. Fargo saw the third man rush up, a bony nose in a bony face, and smash his hand across the girl's cheek.

"Bitch," he rasped as he avoided another kick.

Nick rose, pain still in his face, but his lips drawn back in a grimace of rage. "Take her in the back. We're going to teach her how to be nice," he ordered.

Fargo's eyes scanned the others in the saloon. Most stared into their drinks with determined indifference while a few sneaked quick glances at the three men and the girl. But no one moved to do anything more. They wouldn't, Fargo knew. They were all cut from the same cloth, all losers. Fear was a part of their inaction, as perhaps was some envy and some vicarious enjoyment. It all added up to doing nothing.

"Bastards. Let me go, damn you," Fargo heard the girl shout. She twisted, wriggled, tried to bite, but the three men held her tight as they dragged her across the floor. Two held her arms while the tall, pasty-faced one had seized a handful of her short brown hair and kept her head up. They dragged her toward a closed door at the far end of the saloon.

Fargo let a deep sigh escape him as he rose to his feet. Why the hell was she in the saloon in the first place? he wondered as he eyed the guns the trio wore on their hips. The pasty-faced one wore an army percussion Colt, a slow trigger pull, he grunted inwardly. The other two had Colt Hartford Dragoon pistols, six-shot weapons but heavy in the hand and slow to draw.

"Let the girl go," he said, his voice hardly raised yet carrying with icy clarity.

The three men halted, and the pasty-faced one let go of his grip on the girl's hair as he moved to one side. Frowning, he stared at the big man with the lake-blue eyes and the thick black hair.

"What'd you say?" he growled.

"I said, let the girl go," Fargo repeated.

"Who the hell are you?" the man barked.

"Name's Fargo . . . Skye Fargo," the Trailsman said almost affably.

"You know her?" the pasty-faced one queried.

"Not yet. But I'm getting tired waiting. Let her go, scum," Fargo said, his voice growing crisp.

He saw disbelief slide across the man's pasty face

11

and then spiraling anger. "You're crazy," the man muttered.

"Maybe," Fargo said.

"I'm goin' to shoot your damn head off, mister," the man said.

"You couldn't shoot the ass off an elephant in front of you," Fargo said as his eyes bored into the man's face. But, with his peripheral vision, he saw the man's hand move, his fingers spread out as he brought his arm in line with the holster at his hip. His eyes flicked to the other two men still holding the girl, an instant, silent message. His fingers stiffened and Fargo smiled to himself. Like most stupid gunslingers, the man had given himself away. His hand flashed upward as he went for his gun. It was still curled around the butt of the pistol when Fargo's shot blew his chest apart in a shower of red.

The man fell back into one of the tables, bringing it to the floor with him. But Fargo had already swung the Colt around to the other two. One of them had used the precious split seconds to get his gun out of its holster. He had only raised it halfway into firing position when Fargo's second shot exploded. The stocky figure half-spun around as he swore in pain, clutching at his shoulder as the gun fell from his fingers. He staggered sideways with one hand on his shoulder, fell to his knees, and slumped against one of the tables.

Fargo's gun was on the third man, who had flung himself to the floor with the girl and lay half under her, his gun held against her temple. "Back off or she gets it," he snarled.

Fargo hesitated, his mind racing. Even if he got a bullet into the man, the scum's finger on the trigger would automatically jerk, and the girl was dead. He grimaced and backed a half-dozen steps. The man kept the girl half atop him, the gun against her temple, as he began to push himself backward across the saloon floor toward the door. Fargo, eyes narrowed, the Colt ready to fire, gauged distance, angle, movement, and decided again that it was too risky. The man's finger had only to tighten on the trigger, the muzzle of the gun flat against the girl's temple.

Fargo remained motionless as the man reached the door of the saloon, pushed himself to his feet, and brought the girl up with him. His gun was still against her temple as he backed out of the saloon. Fargo held back until he heard the sound of hoofbeats galloping away. Then he streaked across the dingy little saloon and out onto the street to see the man racing out of town on a brown quarterhorse with the girl on her stomach across the saddle in front of him.

Fargo vaulted onto the magnificent Ovaro as he yanked the reins free of the hitching post with one hand. It only took moments to race to the end of the few buildings that made up the town. He saw the horse streaking on ahead of him through a line of alders. He started after the fleeing horseman, reached the beginning of the alders, and let the man see him rein to a halt. He waited a moment and slowly turned the Ovaro around, aware that the man watched with quick glances. Fargo headed the horse back toward town at a walk, halted again only when the fleeing horseman finally disappeared from sight.

Then he whirled the Ovaro around again and set off across the low hill that rose west of the line of alders. He raced the horse through huge northern red oak, keeping the alders in sight on his left. The hill rose, flattened out, and stayed heavy with the red oak as he turned the horse west toward the alders, which now continued in a line slightly below where he rode. He drew closer to the trees and spotted the fleeing horseman as he moved through open patches. The man had slowed to a trot, but still had the girl lying on her stomach across the saddle.

Fargo swung north, paralleled the horse just below, keeping out of sight in the cover of the red oaks. The man kept riding, plainly taking no chances on being caught. He watched as the alders began to thin, finally ended in a stand of silver balsam that edged a small lake. The purple-gray haze of dusk began to slide across the countryside when Fargo saw the man halt, slide from the horse, and pull the girl from the saddle. He flung her to the ground roughly, and she rolled once. She came up on her elbows to glare back.

Fargo moved the Ovaro down the gentle tree-covered slope as he drew the big Sharps rifle from its saddle holster. He brought the horse to a halt at the end of the red oaks; a short hill of low brush slanted down to where the man faced the girl. "That big bastard thought you were worth shootin' for but not chasin' after," Fargo heard the man say with a snarling laugh.

"Maybe he's still coming," the girl said.

"He quit," the man said. "I kept lookin' back. He didn't show again. Now I'm going to finish what Nick started, you little bitch."

Fargo watched as he moved toward the girl, whose hand came up with a fistful of soil she slammed into the man's face. "Goddamn," the man spit out, blinked, wiped an arm across his face.

The girl was on her feet, running up the hillside, her legs churning as the man started after her. Fargo watched as she glanced back at her pursuer for an instant, broke her momentum, tried to dig in harder, and slipped on a loose stone. She went down on one knee and recovered quickly, but the man was able to get his hand around her left ankle. He slipped as she

14

pulled but held his grip, and the girl went down again.

"Goddamn little bitch," he cursed as he yanked, and she slid down to him.

But she turned as he pulled her, flipped half onto her back, and drove one foot forward down, down. The man turned his face away just in time to avoid the full force of the kick, but he caught part of the blow on the top of his head. It broke his hold on the girl's ankle, and Fargo watched her roll past her attacker, half-fall down the slope, and regain her feet. She was racing for the man's horse, he saw with a smile of admiration. She was one little hellion, full of fight, fire, and guts. He saw the man get to his feet and heard his bellow of rage.

"No, you don't, you goddamn little bitch. I'll kill you, first," the man roared as the girl neared his horse.

Fargo saw her throw a glance back, her eyes wide with fear as she saw the man yank at his gun. But she kept running, the horse hardly a half-dozen yards away. When the man raised his gun and took aim at the girl's running figure, Fargo brought the big Sharps to his shoulder. The rifle shot resounded down the slope as though it were a small, sharp clap of thunder, and the man seemed to go into a strange little dance as he whirled in a half-circle, tottered, and pitched forward to roll down the slope. He stopped rolling almost at the edge of the small lake, and Fargo saw the girl, frozen in place, look back with her eyes wide. She stared at the figure lying lifelessly, then slowly turned her eyes to peer up the hillside as Fargo moved the Ovaro forward into sight and came down to halt in front of her.

She blinked, swallowed, and her pert, snub-nosed face finally relaxed. "I was waiting to feel the bullet when I heard the shot," she said. Fargo swung from the horse and slid the rifle back "Thanks," she added. "Such a dumb little word for so much. I owe you."

He took her in with a long, careful appraisal for the first time and decided his first impression held. She was dammed pretty in her own pugnacious way, her breasts so full and high they pushed proudly into the dark-green shirt, her figure compact and firm. She radiated a kind of energetic vitality even standing still.

"You put up a damn good fight, honey. You're a real hellcat," he finally said. "But going into that saloon was pretty damn dumb. Even the town whores would think twice about going in there."

She met his remarks with her own appraisal as her round, brown eyes took in the chiseled handsomeness of the big man's face, the power in his shoulders and arms.

"What the hell were you doing in there?" Fargo continued, not without a surge of irritation.

"I went to meet you," she said.

Fargo frowned as he stared at the girl's calm face. "You what?" he muttered.

"I was there to meet you," she said again.

His frown deepened, pulling his thick black eyebrows lower. "How the hell did you know I'd be there?" he questioned.

"You were supposed to meet somebody there, weren't you?" she answered.

"Yes, but it sure as hell wasn't you," he snapped.

"I know that," she said with a touch of disdain.

"Who are you? What the hell's this all about?" Fargo asked.

"I'm Trudy Keyser," she said.

"Is that supposed to mean something to me, because it sure as hell doesn't," Fargo growled.

"No. Not yet, anyway," she said.

"Then start explaining, Trudy Keyser. Why'd you come to that rat's nest to meet me?" Fargo questioned.

"I want to hire you. I've real good money for it," the girl said.

"Then you've just wasted your time coming here, and my time saving your little ass. I've got a job," he snapped.

"I know that, too," she said, the touch of disdain in her voice again. "You're on your way to Thief River Junction. This won't interfere with that."

Fargo felt the stab of surprise again. There was surely nothing secret about his destination, but he hadn't expected this feisty, determined girl to know that. "Why won't it interfere?" he questioned cautiously.

"You can teach me on the way," she said.

"Teach you what?" He frowned.

"Teach me everything you know. Teach me to be a trailsman," Trudy Keyser said.

Fargo stared at her round brown eyes, which remained absolutely steady. He shook his head slowly as amazement curled up inside him. "Honey, you are plumb crazy," he said.

2

Her direct eyes flared instantly, and her hands went to her hips to add to the defiant pugnaciousness of her stand. Her firm, compact body almost bristled with anger. "I expected that kind of an answer," she snapped reprovingly.

"Then you can go home happy," Fargo muttered.

"I'm not going home. I'm going with you. You're going to teach me all the things you know," Trudy Keyser said.

"In two weeks?" Fargo half-sneered.

She allowed a curt nod. "All right, I know that's not possible. I'm not an idiot," she said.

"You could've fooled me," Fargo slid in.

She ignored his remark except for a moment when her eyes narrowed. "I learn quickly. You'll teach me as much as I can take in. I want to learn how to track, how to read sign, how to look, listen, see the way you see, understand the way you do. I want to learn all the little things that make you what you are—the very best. I want to see through your eyes, hear as you hear, think as you think, and I'll pay you five hundred dollars to teach me whatever you can."

Fargo felt his brows lift. "That's a damn powerful lot of money, Trudy Keyser," he remarked.

"Yes, and it's all yours for two weeks of teaching," she said.

He studied her pert, pretty face, the round brown eyes that didn't waver under his sharp stare. "Why?" he murmured. "You've got to have yourself a damn good reason."

"I want to become the first woman tracker, the first woman to ride trail," she answered smoothly. "A lot of women are taking their wagons and families through when their menfolk die or are killed. I think they'd like a woman riding trail for them."

Fargo kept the smile inside himself. The answer was glib, waiting on the tip of her tongue, a story made ready to use when the time came. But he kept his thoughts to himself as her voice cut in. "Five hundred dollars, Fargo, for two weeks when you'll be riding anyway. You won't even have to go out of your way. You'll pick up all that money for doing what you were going to do anyway, go to Thief River Junction," Trudy Keyser pushed at him. "It'd be found money."

"You know how to make a case for yourself, I'll give you that," he said.

"Five hundred," she repeated. "I don't see you as a man who'd turn his back on that kind of money."

"Not usually," he agreed.

"Why start now?" she tossed back.

"If I take money, I want to earn it. I don't see myself doing that with this, honey," Fargo said.

"You will," she said calmly.

"Suppose you don't learn a damn thing?" he said.

"That'll be my problem," she answered.

His eyes moved up and down her firm, compact

body and lingered for a moment on the very high breasts that pushed hard into the dark-green shirt. "Suppose I take to hankering for you along the way?" he slid at her.

"That'll be my problem," she echoed calmly.

He allowed a wry smile. "Pretty damn confident of yourself, aren't you?" he said.

"I know what I want to do," she said. "I'll do it. Is it a deal?"

"No, dammit," he barked. "I'll think on it. You're lucky to get that."

"Why?" she shot back.

"You've been a pain in the ass so far, Trudy, honey," Fargo said. "I might have missed my man because I had to go chasing after you."

"You didn't have to," she glared. "But I'm glad you did," she added, her tone softening.

"Force of habit," he grunted as he turned and climbed onto the Ovaro. "I'm going back to the saloon now. I just hope he's still waiting there for me."

"Good, you can take me back with you," Trudy said.

"What the hell for?" Fargo frowned.

"I'm not leaving my horse and gun there," she snapped.

He grimaced and reached down for her. "Come on," he grunted, and swung her onto the pinto behind him. He sent the Ovaro into a trot and felt the soft pressure of her breasts as they rubbed against his back. "How come you knew I was meeting somebody at the Bent Wheel Saloon?" he asked over his shoulder.

"Edgar Tooley told me back in Iowa," she said. "I was looking for you, and I'd heard you just finished breaking trail near Cotoe Plains for him."

Fargo accepted the answer. It fitted. Edgar Tooley

knew where he was headed. "He tell you why I'm going to Thief River Junction?" he asked her.

"Only that you were called in by the sheriff there," Trudy said.

"That's right, Sheriff Covey," Fargo said.

"Why?"

"He's called me to track a man named Jack Towers. Real bad actor, it seems, murdered two people, and he keeps giving them the slip," Fargo said.

"So they called in the very best to track him down," Trudy Keyser said. "Same reason that brought me to you."

Fargo made a snorting sound. "They only want a tough job done. You want the impossible," he said.

"I want as much as I can get. I told you, I'm a quick learn. I'll prove it to you," Trudy said.

He didn't answer as the handful of houses came into sight, and he hurried the horse through the excuse for a town until he reached the saloon. "There he is," Trudy cried out happily, and gestured to a dark-brown, sturdy-legged horse at the hitching post.

"He's got quarterhorse in him," Fargo said.

"And thoroughbred," Trudy said as she slid from the Ovaro. "I'll wait here," she said beside her horse.

"Give me ten minutes," Fargo ordered as he strode into the saloon. The bartender looked up as he entered, and his face grew apprehensive at once. But he glanced quickly away under Fargo's hard stare. Fargo walked around the edges of the tables where everyone in the dim place could see him, and made his way to a corner table. He had just sat down when a middle-aged man with wispy gray hair approached him.

"Fargo?" the man asked tentatively, and the Trailsman nodded. "The description they gave me

21

fits," the man said as he eased himself into a chair. "Will Clements."

Fargo acknowledged the introduction with a curt nod. "What have you got for me?" he asked.

"They told me you'd pay. Times are kinda hard," Clements said, a note of whining in his voice.

"If it's worth anything," Fargo answered.

"It is," the man said. "I worked with Jack Towers down in Wisconsin. He drove freight for A. E. Howard. He's a young, quiet feller, never took him for the killin' kind. Never saw a man with such a good feel for horses. He could tell a horse was tirin' before the horse knew it."

"That's very nice. I hope you don't expect pay if that's all you've got," Fargo said.

"I've more," the man said. "Jack Towers always carried two extra canteens of water on every trip."

"Go on," Fargo said, coming to attention at once.

"Seems he was sick when he was a youngster, some kind of high fever that burned his insides, and now he can't go very long without water," Will Clements said.

"Anything else?" Fargo questioned.

"He wears a special heel on his right foot," the man said. "Without it, he's got a little limp."

Fargo reached into his pocket and put five silver dollars on the table. "You've earned your money," he said, and watched the man quickly scoop the coins into a torn pocket. Fargo's eyes went to the doorway as Will Clements began to walk away, and he saw Trudy's compact figure enter. She strode directly to the bar, and Fargo saw the bartender's eyes widen.

"You again, girlie? Didn't you get enough before?" the bartender growled.

"I want my Walker," she said.

"I don't know anything about your gun," the bartender said, and turned away from her.

"You're a damn liar," Trudy shot back, and Fargo had to smile. She was right, the man was too quick to turn away from her. "The gun was thrown under one of your tables. You took it when things settled down. I want it back."

"Go to hell, sister," the bartender said. "And get out of my saloon."

"You give me my gun, or you'll be sorry," Trudy snapped.

"Get out," the bartender sneered. "Don't come back."

Fargo stayed in the chair and watched Trudy spin on her heel and stride from the saloon, her pert, pretty face set in determined fury. The bartender's snorting laugh said that he thought Trudy was going off in defeat. He was in for a surprise, Fargo wagered silently as he waited, sitting back in his chair to enjoy the luxury of being a spectator. His eyes were on the double doors of the entrance as they smashed open and the dark-brown horse burst into the saloon. Trudy sat in the saddle with a rifle in her hands. She raised the rifle and fired off two shots as she rode the horse at the bar. The bottles on the wall behind the bartender exploded in a shower of glass, and Fargo saw the bartender, his jaw hanging open, dive down behind the bar.

Ordinarily he'd have been safe there, but atop the horse Trudy reined up alongside the bar, she looked directly down at him over the bartop. She raised the rifle again. "The next one blows your lying head off unless I get my gun," she said, and Fargo's glance took in the other customers crouched under the tables.

"Jesus, all right," he heard the bartender's voice

answer. "Just take it easy, lady," the man said, respect mingling with the fear in his voice.

"The gun, dammit," Trudy snapped, and Fargo saw the bartender's head appear over the edge of the bar as he pulled himself to his feet. He reached into a shelf under the bar, brought the Walker out, and carefully handed it up to Trudy, who still held the rifle aimed at his chest. She leaned over, took the gun, stuck it into her belt, and backed the dark-brown horse out of the bar, letting the horse push the doors open with his rump. When she was fully out, Fargo rose to his feet and met the shock still in the bartender's eyes.

"Some women are harder to handle than others," Fargo commented as he walked from the saloon.

Trudy was astride her horse waiting for him, the rifle back in its saddle holster.

"That bartender's a lucky man," Fargo said as he swung onto the Ovaro. "I'm just not sure of the reasons."

"What's that mean?" Trudy said as she swung alongside him, and he trotted up the street.

"Either he's lucky because you can't shoot straight or because you can," Fargo said.

She said nothing but rode with a tiny glower on her face as they left town. They'd gone about a quarter-mile out when she reined up suddenly beside a field covered with dried-out stalks of corn that rose stiffly into the air like so many soldiers in tattered uniforms. He watched her round-cheeked face set itself as she drew the revolver from her belt and took aim at the first stalk of corn of the nearest row. She fired, and the top of the stalk blew away. Fargo watched as she moved the gun, took aim again, and the top of the second stalk of corn disintegrated. She blew away six of the stalks, each shot aimed and on target. Her eyes

24

went to the big man sitting beside her when she finished, a hint of smug triumph in their brown orbs.

"That answer you?" she asked, reloading the gun.

"More or less," he said.

"More or less? Is that all?" Trudy flared as she put the gun back into her belt.

"I'm a hard man to impress." Fargo smiled.

"Can you do better?" she snapped.

Fargo let the smile stay for a moment longer, then his hand snapped down to the holster at his side. It came up with the big Colt firing, six shots fired so quickly the sound blended into one, and Trudy Keyser watched the next six stalks of corn blow apart.

"That answer your question?" Fargo echoed.

She peered at him as he reloaded. "Very impressive," she said, as she pulled her gun out again and fired at the next six cornstalks, this time as Fargo had done, with hardly a pause to aim in between. He watched three of the stalks disintegrate, one dip sideways and two remain untouched. He caught the glower in her pert face as she glanced at him. "Better than most would do," she muttered.

"I'll go along with that," Fargo agreed, and her face softened. "You're good. I'm better." He grinned.

"I expect that," Trudy snapped. "That's why I'm here." Her nose wrinkled and the line of freckles seemed to dance.

"Where'd you learn to shoot like that?" Fargo asked as he moved the Ovaro forward and Trudy swung alongside him.

"My pa taught me. He said a girl ought to know how to shoot," she answered.

"Especially one with your sass," Fargo said. He put the Ovaro into a gentle trot, and Trudy lingered behind. He knew the question was hanging on her lips, and he'd thought about the answer. The truth was that she intrigued him with her pugnacious determination. Not that he believed the story she'd had ready for him. But she had reasons, strong ones, he was certain of that much. She wasn't the kind for whims or fool notions. Having her along would make the trip interesting as well as profitable, and his eyes narrowed as he thought about the money she had offered. Not the kind a man turned away without a damn good reason. He planned a visit with Alva Brown, and he knew damn well Alva could use some of that kind of money. He smiled as he recalled how his pa always said that found money ought to be shared. He cast a glance at Trudy as she rode close behind him.

She had called it found money and she'd been right. It was exactly that to him, and he really had no reason to turn her down. Except one, he grunted to himself, but he'd let her do the deciding on that, though he had little doubt what she'd decide. Still his own integrity demanded he tell her the truth of it. So when she called the question, it didn't really cut into his thoughts. It was more like opening a door.

"Are we going on together, Fargo?" Trudy asked, and he halted and met the challenge in her eyes.

"There are a few things you ought to know first," he said. "Especially if you're spending big money."

"I'm listening," she said.

"Most folks can't ever track, because it's not just learning. You don't just look, hear, smell. You have to have the feeling inside you. Some call it a special sensitivity, some call it instinct. I call it having a special kind of wildness inside you. But call it whatever you will, it's the feeling inside that makes you see right, hear right, smell right. Without the feeling inside, all the learning won't do you a damn bit of good. Without the instinct, you're wasting time and money," he said harshly, but her snub nose stayed tilted upward, her brown eyes unwavering.

"I've the feeling," she said without hesitation. "What else?"

"I'm making one stop along the way, to visit a woman I know, Alva Brown. I promised I'd come see her if I were ever up this way," he said.

She tossed him a half-shrug. "Go ahead. I won't ask to watch," she said snappishly.

"Good," he returned, and kept the smile inside himself. She was one quick-tongued little package.

"Anything more?" she questioned.

"One question," he said, and she waited. "What're you sitting there for? You've a heap of learning to do," he said, and put the Ovaro into a canter. He heard Trudy's half-squeal of delight and she caught up to him in moments, her pert prettiness bright with satisfaction. She handed him a roll of bills, and he pushed them into his saddlebag.

"Aren't you going to count it?" Trudy asked.

"I would with some people. Not with you," he answered.

"But you don't know me that well," she protested.

"Reading people is like reading trail. There are some signs that never go wrong," he said. "You're not the cheating kind."

She cast an interested glance at him. "What kind am I?" she asked.

"Too much sass and spit for your own good." He laughed. "You go after what you want. You'd fight, maybe even kill, but you wouldn't cheat."

She looked away and rode in silence beside him as he turned the Ovaro north and settled into an easy pace. His gaze reached out at the land that lay ahead: the wild northwest Minnesota Territory, a land both rich and harsh, hills made of good tree cover and sparkling lakes that suddenly appeared as if by magic. It was a land of tamaracks, silver spruce and balsams, northern pine and black oak, pin cherry and white birch, of thick, wiry brush and good green grass. The Chippewa rode the northwest land, sometimes the Yankton Dakota and the Western Cree, but mostly the Assiniboin. The wind could caress in this land and it could howl down from the Canada border with killing fury. Nature came at you with the suddenness of a redman's arrow and death hid behind its beauty.

He led the way across hills grown thick with pine and silver maple, and his eyes flicked to Trudy. "You're just riding," he barked, and surprise flooded her face. "Lesson one. You don't ever just ride. You ride and look, always, until it becomes an automatic habit." She nodded, a chastened expression touching her face. "Start now," he ordered. "Tell me if you see anything, especially wearing feathers." He rode on, and Trudy stayed beside him as he guided the horses up the slow side of the first hill, the tree-thick sides of the facing hills in front and to the left. Trudy rode in silence for the better part of a half-hour when he tossed a questioning glance at her.

"Nothing," she said.

"Try again. There are three Chippewa moving down the side of the hill to your left," he said. Her mouth dropped open, and she flung a glance of shock at him before her eyes went to the hillside. "They're out of sight at the moment, but they're there," he said.

"I didn't see anything. I was looking," Trudy protested. "I didn't see anybody."

"Because you were looking for them, trying to pick someone out of all those trees and branches. You don't find anything that way, especially an Indian," Fargo said.

"Then how did you see them?" Trudy frowned.

"The way you'll learn to see. You look for other things first. Think of it as trying to see the wind. You can't, but you can see where the wind blows. You watch the leaves, the trees, the brush. All those things move when something brushes through them. You watch for movement and follow it down. The movement gives you your fix."

"How do you know it isn't just the wind blowing the leaves?" she questioned.

"Wind blows through trees with a long, sweeping movement. It's an altogether different motion. You can't mistake the two," he said.

She nodded understanding, and her eyes scanned the hillside as she listened. She rode slowly beside him and suddenly her words snapped out, filled with excitement. "There, halfway down by those balsams. I see them," she said, and Fargo glimpsed the three redmen moving downhill.

"Very good," he said, and there was no patronizing in his words. She did pick up quickly, he noted, and he led the way up the hill to the top where it flattened out with a thick cover of silver maple.

"It'll be dark soon. Let's make camp," he said, and halted in a small glen. He dismounted, unsaddled the pinto, and made a small fire, just large enough to warm the beef jerky from his saddlebag. Trudy had her own dried beef and sat across from him, the fire's glowing softening her pert face. But even relaxed, she brimmed with vitality, an eagerness that spilled from her with the enthusiasm of a six-year-old. But her firm breasts and very compact, full figure quickly dispelled that illusion. There was a sexiness to her vitality, he decided, a pure, unmannered vibrancy.

"Tell me how to read hoofprints when you're tracking somebody?" Trudy said.

"Finish your beef and be quiet," he growled.

"Why? I can't afford to waste a minute. You said so yourself. I've a lot to learn," she replied.

"Not this way," he grunted, and she frowned back. "Trailing is like making love to a woman. You don't learn to do it by talking about it. You only learn by doing it. There's no other way."

She cast a slow glance at him, a hint of tartness in it. "You're an expert in that also?" she remarked.

"Let's say I've had no complaints," Fargo answered.

He saw her carefully keep her face from showing anything. "You get what you wanted from that man you met in the saloon?" she asked, changing the subject abruptly.

"Enough," he said.

"You ever meet this Jack Towers?" she asked.

"No, but I've a description of him, and Sheriff Covey will be going with me," Fargo said.

"I thought you liked to work alone," Trudy said.

"I'll do the tracking. He'll do the arresting," Fargo said. "Now let's get some sleep."

He rose, took down his bedroll, spread it out, and watched her put hers down nearby. He began to pull off clothes in the last glow of the fire, and she stayed to take in the muscled beauty of his torso before scooping up a bag and going into the trees. He was inside his bedroll when she reappeared wearing a man's wool shirt as a nightgown. It hung oversize on her, covered most of her, but let him see nicely curved, strong calves.

"I don't like nightgowns," she explained almost truculently as she slid into her bedroll with quick modesty and the last of the fire went out.

He lay awake for a spell in the silence of the night and listened to the soft sounds from inside the trees.

"What was that?" Trudy asked, a touch of alarm in her voice at a soft, susurrant sound.

"Deer," Fargo said.

She fell silent until, a little while later, another sound rustled through the woods. "Deer?" she offered.

"Weasel. Maybe ferret," Fargo murmured.

"Sounds the same as the deer," Trudy said.

"Deer rustle leaves. Weasels rustle brush," Fargo growled. "Go to sleep." He turned on his side, the big Colt near his hand, and pulled sleep around him. The night remained quiet, and he woke with the morning sun to hear Trudy dressing in the trees. He pulled clothes on and saddled the Ovaro as she emerged buttoning a green-checked shirt, eagerness shining in her pert face. They breakfasted in a bush of wild plums and mulberry trees, and as he led the way across the stretch of flat high land, he found a set of hoofprints recent enough to read in the loose soil.

"What do you see?" he asked Trudy.

She peered hard at the tracks. "Four horses," she said. "Riding hard."

He followed the tracks with her for a hundred yards. "Running or chasing?" he asked.

"I don't know." She frowned.

"Chasing, probably mavericks," Fargo said.

"How can you tell?"

"See any tracks coming up behind?" Fargo asked, and she nodded understanding. He rode on farther and slowed. "See anything more?" he asked, and she shook her head no. "Their horses are tiring," he said, and her glance questioned. He pointed to the tracks. "Their strides are shortening. They'll have to rein up soon." He motioned and she followed as he went into a canter to where the hoofprints ended in a wheel of tracks. "They didn't catch whatever they were chasing," he said. "Now find us some water."

"How?" Trudy frowned.

He pointed to a flight of swallows winging downward on the other side of a low rise. "Birds fly to water in the morning, away from it in the evening." he said. He rode on, and they found a small pond on the other side of the rise where they filled canteens and let the horses drink. A thick forest of white pine rose on the other side of the pond. "I'm going in there," Fargo said. "You find me. Give me five minutes' start."

She nodded and he rode around the pond to disappear into the thick pine forest. Once inside, he guided the Ovaro across the bed of pine needles that covered the forest floor. It was like riding on a soft carpet as the horse pressed marks into the mass of pine needles. But the deep bed of pine needles was a resilient carpet that sprang back in minutes to leave not the hint of a hoofprint. He moved another fifty yards and halted behind the thick trunk of an old pine. Trudy came into sight soon, riding slowly, peering at the ground, her face wreathed in a frown. She turned her horse left, then right, searched aimlessly. "Damn," he heard her mutter.

"Over here," he called, and her head snapped up, short brown hair swinging from side to side. Chagrin held her face as she rode up to him.

"I lost the tracks. The damn pine needles," she said.

"You just learned two things at once: first, pine needles are a perfect place to hide your tracks; second, when you can't find tracks you look for other things. Tracks are only one way to follow a trail," Fargo told her.

"Such as?" Trudy queried.

Fargo gestured to the ends of the thin, young pine branches. "Snapped off by my horse moving through; maple or hickory would also have the leaves brushed back and bruised. That's what you look for when you can't find tracks. It's as certain a trail as hoofprints," he told her, and he could almost hear the clicking of her mind as she stored away his words. He cantered on, and she followed, reining up in the deep of the forest after a while.

"You go on. Let's try again," she said. He turned the Ovaro and moved into the woods as he had before, staying on the deep, thick carpet of pine needles until he finally halted and waited. She gave him the time again, and he finally saw her appear through the trees. There was no unsteadiness in her movements this time. She guided the dark-brown horse directly at him and reined up when she found him. He nodded in approval at her slightly smug smile. She picked up damn fast, he murmured inwardly. She had the instinct. He turned and went on, and she followed him through the pine forest to where it ended in a heavy stand of silver maple.

The day had drifted into midafternoon, and he found a deep stream and showed her how to use the water to throw off pursuers, demonstrated how to brush over tracks at the banks, and each time he gave an object lesson that she'd remember. "But taking to a stream or a river has been tried with you following. I'm sure you found some way around it," Trudy said.

"You ride through the water and watch the banks. Most clever men hide their tracks going in. Very few do it when they leave. You keep your eyes open and you'll usually see where they left the water and went back on land," he answered.

"How do you know whether to go upstream or

down?'' she asked, and he had to smile. Her questions were sharp and to the heart of it.

"That's tricky, but there's a way," he answered. "Watch as I go into the stream. Let's say I've brushed away my tracks from in the water and now I ride off in the stream or river. It's almost certain I'll go off fast." To illustrate, he sent the Ovaro into a canter through the water, halted, and returned down to where Trudy waited. "Look along the edge of the bank there," he said. "You can see the water marks higher up on the bank than they are downstream. If I'd raced off downstream, they'd be highest on the downstream banks."

She nodded, her eyes narrowed. "What about leaving the stream without showing prints. Can it be done?" she asked.

"It can be done, though most riders on the run don't take the time to be that careful," Fargo said. "You find a flat rock near the water's edge and take your horse up on it. No hoofprints on rock."

She regarded him thoughtfully. "I'm sure that's been tried on you and you weren't fooled," she said. "Why?"

He laughed. "A horse leaving a stream usually carries a little bit of stream bottom in his hooves, a trace of mud or wet clay. That's what you look for on the rock and that's what most riders never stop to think about."

Her eyes stayed on him and a tiny smile of appreciation touched her lips. "Really remarkable. Little things most men wouldn't even think about," she murmured more to herself than to him.

"Little things add up to big things," Fargo said.

"And you add up to something special," Trudy said. "The Trailsman. I know now why they call you that. You've made me see as I've never seen before.

34

It's like opening up the world in a different way. It's kind of breathtaking."

"Maybe because it's coming at you all at once," he said.

"I wouldn't detect a touch of modesty, would I?" Trudy slid at him.

"You sure as hell wouldn't, honey," Fargo muttered, and put the pinto into a trot. Trudy came alongside, her back straight, the high breasts bouncing up and down.

"We've time for more today," she said excitedly, and he laughed, her eagerness infectious.

When the day finally drew to an end, he had taught her how to use her ears as eyes, how to listen and distinguish sounds. But most of all, he'd taught her how to listen to silence.

"It's a sign," Fargo told her. "The forest isn't a quiet place at all. It only seems that way to those whose ears have been dulled by man-made noise: hammering, sawing, shouting, the creaking of wagons, the clatter of dishes, all the noise people surround themselves with. But the forest isn't silent. It clicks, chirps, flutters, buzzes, creaks, whistles, growls, rustles, whispers, patters, caws, twitters, hums, and so on. The hills and plains are no different. But when they're suddenly still, it means something. When there's silence, when nothing flies up, runs, scurries, flutters, or calls, there's danger near. Everything is in hiding, waiting, aware. You'd better be too."

When night came, she ate in thoughtful silence, saying hardly a word as they made bedrolls ready. She slipped inside hers, the long man's shirt flipping up to let him glimpse a length of nice, firm leg.

"You're awful quiet," he finally commented.

"Thinking," she murmured.

"About what?"

"About too many things," she said almost crossly. "Good night. And thanks."

"For what?" he asked.

"For all you're teaching me," she said.

"Hell, that's what you're paying for," he said.

She sat up and looked across at him, and he saw tiny points pushing into the wool shirt at the tips of the firm breasts. "But you're doing it well. You know how to teach, and nobody can buy that. I'm grateful to you for it," she said. She lay down at once, turned her back at him with a flounce, almost as if she were angry at herself. Or at something.

Fargo lay still and listened to her fall asleep. She was full of surprises, he smiled to himself. He'd do some probing on his own soon, he decided, and closed his eyes.

The night passed quietly, and the day came in bright and warm. He found a lake, shimmering and inviting, nestled behind a line of white birch. "It'd save time if we didn't take turns," he mentioned casually.

She stared into space for a moment and brought her direct eyes to his. "I'm not ready for that yet," she said.

"I like that word 'yet.' " He laughed and turned the Ovaro, leaving her alone.

She had just finished dressing when he moved back to the lake, flung off clothes, and dived in. She had taken her horse and gone into the trees but not as far as he had, Fargo smiled as he heard the horse blow air. He swam, rolled in the cool, refreshing water, and finally clambered onto the bank and dried himself with a towel from his saddlebag. He left his shirt off and let the sun dry his torso as he climbed onto the Ovaro, and Trudy came up to ride beside him.

He found a valley and taught her how to watch

ridges and make use of the long shadows special to valleys. Later, on a flat-wooded area, he tested her again on the things he'd taught her, and found himself admiring how well she had learned. When night came and they bedded down, she grew quiet once again and her "good night" held a strange tone, a mixture of softness and crossness. Trudy Keyser was proving to be a far more apt pupil than he'd ever imagined—and more complex. More than that, he realized how much he enjoyed teaching her, watching her pick up so quickly on things, her pugnacious vitality as engaging as her snub-nosed prettiness.

But he noted a pattern had begun to form: the days filled with her cheerful, eager enthusiasm; the nights turning her almost instantly quiet with that strange combination of softness and an edge of hostility. It was almost as if she were two different persons, and he found himself intrigued by both. It was on a warm afternoon when she surprised him again. He'd thrown her the task of tracking him through a rock-rimmed maze of passages with a loose-stone footing, and she had done so with ease.

"You're a damn sight better than I ever expected," he told her. She gave a happy little chortling sound as she spontaneously threw her arms around him. He felt the soft firmness of her breasts press against his chest. He expected her to pull away quickly, but she stayed and lifted her face to his.

"You're a damn-sight better teacher than I expected," she said. He leaned down, found her lips with his, and pressed gently, tasting the honey sweetness of her. Her lips, half-parted, didn't answer, nor did they pull away. He pressed a fraction harder, and finally she stepped back.

"Let's ride. There's plenty of time left to learn more," she said abruptly.

"There's more than one kind of teaching," Fargo said.

"I'll stick to the kind I'm getting," she said, and swung onto her horse.

He laughed and led the way on, brought her into a hillside of thick brush and a line of low rocks that edged the passage they rode. She was on the side nearest the line of rocks when he saw her suddenly fight her horse. As he watched, the horse pulled back, half-reared, and she pulled hard on the bit, tightened her grip, and yanked his head around as he snorted nervously.

"Leave him alone," Fargo snapped sharply, and drew a surprised glance from Trudy as she relaxed her hold of the reins. The horse backed up at once, tossed his head, and blew air.

"He just suddenly started to act up for no reason," she said.

"Wrong," Fargo growled. "Most riders make the mistake you just did. They usually pay for it in some way. Pay attention to your horse, especially if you want to be a trailsman. He'll sense things before you do, pick up things you don't. When he suddenly acts up, he's telling you something. Maybe something harmless spooked him, but then maybe not. The point is you pay attention to him."

"What brought this on just now?" Trudy frowned.

"I don't know, but we'd better find out," Fargo said, and moved the Ovaro toward the line of rocks where Trudy's horse had shied. He saw the Ovaro's ears flatten and felt the instant tension in the horse as the animal's legs stiffened. Fargo held the reins loosely and the horse backed away from the rocks.

"Rattlers, in those rocks," Fargo said. "A horse will always sense a rattler even before he hears it." He backed the pinto away from the rocks and rode on alongside the brush as Trudy followed. When they'd passed the spot, she came up beside him.

They reached a flat, open area of almost grassless soil where more than one set of hoofprints crossed one another. "How can you tell how old hoofprints are when you're trailing them?" Trudy asked.

"Fresh prints have firm edges, and they're usually damp in the centers where the earth has pressed down. The drier they are and the more crumbly the edges, the older they are," Fargo answered. He dismounted and had her run her hands over the hoofprints. When she finished, he remounted, and his eyes were narrowed. "You know, Trudy Keyser, you seem awfully interested in how to trail for somebody who wants to lead wagon trains," he commented.

Her face remained composed, and she answered with casual calm. "Doesn't it all hang together? You never know what you might get into leading a train," she said.

"Maybe," he allowed, and smiled inwardly. Her answer held the same glibness her original reasons had, and she was as quick at clicking off replies as she was at learning. But he was more certain than ever that she handed him a lot less than the truth. "Let's ride," he said aloud, and led the way across low hills, watching the distant sky where cumulus clouds had begun to gather.

When night fell, she became silent, once again a troubled, brooding quality in her pert face. But she sat close to him as they ate, and the quick glances she tossed his way were deep and soft. She went to sleep in silence except for a murmured "good night," and the next day she plunged herself eagerly into the morning's lessons. But the night brought the silent withdrawal he had begun to expect with increasing curiosity, and this time he sat back against a birch as they finished the jerky.

"You afraid of the dark?" he asked casually.

"No." She frowned. "Why?"

"Comes night you shrink into yourself. You become a different person," he said.

"I'm just tired," she said in dismissal.

He laughed. "You're quick with answers, even bullshit ones," he commented, and saw the glower come into her face.

"That's all it is," she snapped as she rose and laid out her bedroll.

"Try again, honey," Fargo said.

"I answered you. I suppose you've got your own ideas," she tossed back.

"A couple," he said.

She straightened up and glared at him. "This ought to be fascinating," she said tartly. "Let's have them, by all means."

"One, something's eating at you. You can handle it in the day by keeping yourself busy. When night comes, it rushes over you, and you can't keep it away," he said.

"Nonsense," she said with disdain. "What's the other one?"

"When night comes and it's bedroll time, you have to fight hard with yourself to keep from doing what you really want to do," Fargo said.

"And what's that?"

"Climb into my bedroll. The only way you can handle it is to close into yourself," he answered.

"Oh, you like that explanation, don't you?" Trudy said, hands on her hips.

"Which one's right?" Fargo asked calmly.

"Neither, dammit. They're both wrong," she flung

back as she scooped up her nightshirt and stomped into the trees.

Fargo undressed and was lying in his bedroll when she returned, her nose high in the air. She climbed into her bedroll, turned her back to him, and he could feel her simmering anger. He smiled as the fire went out. She'd called both his explanations wrong, and he'd been certain one or the other was right. Now he wondered if perhaps they were both right, more than one shadow pushing at her. He promised himself he'd know before they reached Thief River.

3

He began to teach her how to read and trail animal tracks the next day. "Why?" she questioned with a frown.

"Remember what I told you about paying attention to your horse?" he asked. "You need to pay attention to every other animal too. Beaver tracks can lead you to water. A bear can take you to good fruit trees, a lynx can take you to where you can catch a dinner of rabbit, an elk can lead you to a trail opened through heavy woods. But more than that, you learn to read wolf tracks or cougar prints so you suddenly don't find that you're the one being hunted."

He spent the entire day at it as they rode north, going off on three or four side forays to follow a set of wolf tracks and a marten trail. As he had come to expect, Trudy had taken in a lot of learning by the time the day began to nod toward dusk. The land had led into a place of granite formations, and Fargo pointed to a row of tracks that were printed into the loose, dry soil at the edge of the rocks. "Cougar," he muttered.

"They look like lynx tracks only bigger," Trudy said.

"There's another difference. The spaces between the pads are tighter," Fargo pointed out as Trudy reined up where the tracks disappeared.

"Where'd he go?" She frowned.

"Bounded up on the rocks," Fargo said as he dismounted. "The only good way to track a cougar is on foot. He'll go from soil to rocks and back again, and you have to follow. Most times a horse can't do it, and more important, horses are afraid of cougars. Most won't even track a cougar."

He left the Ovaro and clambered along the low rocks on foot, Trudy following, until he paused and pointed to where the cougar tracks appeared again on a strip of loose soil between the rocks. He followed the tracks for a little longer with Trudy until he halted. "This cat's just prowling around, moving easy, a good, relaxed stride. See how even the prints stay?" He went on a few yards more until the tracks disappeared again at the slope of a smooth rock. "He went up there," he said.

"How do you know?" Trudy questioned.

Fargo pointed with one finger. "There, those little bits of dirt on the rock near the bottom. Left by his forepaws when he made his first jump." Fargo turned and started to retrace steps back to where they'd left the horses. "A cougar is just about the hardest thing there is to track," he told her when they reached the horses. "It'll be dark soon. We'd best make camp."

"The cougar, he'll just prowl around here?" she asked.

"More than likely, especially if he has a kill stashed away someplace near here," Fargo said. He rode on until he found a hollow between two granite slabs just as dark lowered its curtain. He made a fire of a few twigs, and Trudy grew silent as they ate, glowering as she felt Fargo's eyes studying her.

"I'm tired, that's all it is," she said defensively.

"Whatever you say, Trudy," Fargo agreed.

"Which really means you don't believe me," Trudy sniffed.

"Go to the head of the class." Fargo smiled.

She looked away and leaned back on her elbows, her breasts pushing the shirt tight, filling the fabric with round contours. "How long before we reach Thief River?" she asked almost sullenly.

"A week or so, I'd guess," Fargo said. "Plenty of time for you to learn more."

The sullenness stayed in her face as she rose and set out her bedroll. He did the same with his as she went behind one of the rocks with the nightshirt. He was undressed and in his bedroll when she returned, her face still wreathed in a glower.

"It's not enough time," she muttered as she knelt down on her bedroll. "I need much more practice. I want to be really good."

"You're damn good now," Fargo said. "You've surprised the hell out of me."

"I want to be better," Trudy said, and he saw her head come up, her pert face stare across at him. "Forget about the sheriff and that man they want you to find. Stay and teach me more. I'll find some more money."

Fargo shook his head. "No way I can do that," he told her.

"Just don't go. Forget about it. Stay here and teach me," Trudy repeated.

"Teach you just trailblazing?" Fargo questioned.

Her lips tightened. "Maybe not. I'm not sure," she said.

Fargo laughed. "Doesn't matter. I can't stay," he said. "I agreed to do a job. I won't go back on that."

"You mean you don't want to," Trudy sniffed.

"I mean I won't. That's not the same thing," Fargo corrected.

"It is to me," she said crossly.

Fargo's eyes narrowed at her as she stared down at her clenched hands. "Why is becoming a trailsman so damn important?" he asked. "You trying to prove something? To your pa?" he prodded.

Her glance was quick and sharp. "Why do you say that?" she murmured.

"It happens often enough, sons trying to prove themselves to fathers. Daughters, too, especially ones full of spit and sass," Fargo answered.

He watched her as she pursed her lips thoughtfully. "I gave you my reasons. You ought to try believing people," she said.

"You ought to try telling the truth," Fargo shot back.

She turned her back to him and lay down with an angry thud. He lay back, certain he had hit close to the heart of her inner shadows. He closed his eyes when he heard her sit up, push out of her bedroll. He opened his eyes and saw her half-roll over to him, and her mouth came down hard on his, her lips sweet-soft yet angry, trembling, quivering, and he felt the fleeting taste of her tongue. She pulled away as abruptly as she had kissed him.

"Just so's you'll know what you might be missing," she threw at him, and rolled over to her bedroll to disappear inside it. Fargo lay back again and smiled. The next week promised to be even more interesting than the first. He pulled sleep around himself as he closed his eyes again and the night remained quiet.

When he woke, the morning sun filtered through a

gray haze, and his glance went to Trudy's bedroll. It was empty, and he lay still and listened for the sound of her dressing behind the rocks. When he heard nothing, he sat up, a tiny frown creasing his brow. He listened again and still heard only silence, and he began to pull on clothes. His eyes darted to the horses and saw her dark-brown mare beside the Ovaro, but the frown on his brow suddenly dug deeper as he spotted the empty rifle holster alongside her saddle.

He rose, strapped on his gun belt as he scanned the ground near her bedroll and found her footprints at once. He cursed softly as he followed their trail where she'd left the campsite and gone up along the passages of loose soil. The cougar prints came into sight, and Fargo's mouth became a thin, angry line across his chiseled countenance. Trudy's prints followed the cougar tracks up a gentle slope toward the higher rocks, and he cursed her damn-fool, headstrong stubbornness.

The cougar's tracks vanished beside a pair of low boulders, but Trudy's prints went on where the pathway dropped sharply. He saw her prints, sliding marks now, where she had gone down the sharp drop. She'd thought to pick up the big cat's prints farther on again at the other side of the drop, and he let himself slide downward.

"Little fool," he swore aloud as he hit the bottom of the drop and trotted after her prints. She had been right in figuring that the cougar would come down from the rocks on the other side; he saw as the big cat's tracks appeared again. Trudy was trotting, hurrying after the tracks as they led upward again.

Fargo halted, dropped down on one knee, and peered hard at the cougar's tracks. "Shit," he muttered as he rose and hurried on, his lips pulled back in a grimace as he studied the tracks. The loose soil

46

ended in a long, flat slope of rock, and Trudy's prints turned and vanished as she went up the slope. Fargo followed, broke into a run as he climbed the rock slope. He was nearing the top when Trudy's scream rent the morning stillness, mingled with the piercing hiss of the cougar.

Fargo yanked the Colt from its holster as the cougar's snarls shivered through the air. He reached the top of the slope where it leveled onto a ledge and saw Trudy's prostrate form, the cougar standing over her. He fired, not daring to waste time in aiming, his objective only to get the big cat off her. The cougar whirled as the shots slammed into the rock behind him, then it hissed and disappeared over a boulder with one tremendous leap as Fargo raced to the still form. He reached Trudy and saw she was unconscious, lying facedown, the back of her shirt hanging in shreds with a long stripe of red running from each tear. Her rifle lay nearby, and he saw that she'd never had the chance to bring it around to shoot as the cougar sprang from above and in back of her.

Fargo lifted her carefully, put her over his shoulder, and picked up the rifle with one hand. He moved slowly down the rock slope and heard her soft moan. He was at the bottom of the slope when he felt her stir. She made a little sound that became a groan, then words.

"Be quiet," he said harshly, felt her go limp again over his shoulder. When he reached the campsite, he put her down gently on her stomach and she half-turned her head to peer at him with the pain in her eyes. "Don't move," he ordered, hurried to the Ovaro, and dug deep into the saddlebag to bring out a cork-stoppered vial.

He rushed back to where Trudy lay and lifted the remains of the back of her shirt over her shoulders, tore off strips of the material, and used them to clean away the blood from the edges of the claw marks. Though she cried out in pain at his touch, she managed to lie still.

"You're lucky," Fargo said. "They're not too deep. I've seen a cougar's claws lay a man's backbone open." She gave a moan as he began to apply the salve from the vial, rubbing it gently down the length of each claw mark.

"Yarrow and comfrey with aloe vera mixed in as a disinfectant. Does small miracles," Fargo said as he gently applied the salve. He used his strong yet sensitive fingers to coat each claw wound and spread the salve across the rest of her back where bruised muscles would knot in pain. When he finished, he lay pieces of her torn shirt over the wounds. "You'll have to stay on your stomach for now," Fargo said.

"He was about to really tear into me when you got there, wasn't he?" Trudy murmured.

"I'd guess so," Fargo said, and started to pull his arm back when her hand reached out, closed over his forearm. She drew his arm to her and pressed her forehead down on it as her fingers clenched over his hand.

"I'm sorry," she murmured, her head on his arm. "You said a cougar was about the hardest thing there is to track."

"I didn't say you were ready to do it," he growled, and her hand tightened on his.

"I know, but I wanted to do it," she said, not lifting her head.

"It was more than that," Fargo said coldly. "You were steaming about last night, so you decided to do some more proving."

She was silent for a moment. "I'm sorry," she said

finally. "I owe you again. I didn't mean to cause trouble."

"Thank God for small favors," Fargo grunted, and he peered down at her round-cheeked face, which had turned to rest one cheek on his arm. The pertness was drained from it. Even the freckles across her nose seemed pale. "Rest. Close your eyes. You'll feel better by tonight," he said.

"Where are you going?" she asked as he drew his arm away.

"Get us something fresh for dinner," he said, and patted the firm, round rear. Her eyes closed and she was asleep before he rode the Ovaro out of the rocky hollow.

He rode west into thick brush. He spotted Indian pony tracks moving away and rode on. He took the Sharps from its saddle holster as he made his way through heavy underbrush. He was ready, the rifle under one arm, when the pair of ruffed grouse took wing. He brought one down with a clean shot, retrieved the bird, and rode back to the rock hollow.

Trudy was still hard asleep, and he made a fire, steamed and singed the feathers from the bird, rigged up a spit, and began to cook dinner over a low, slow fire. It was late afternoon when Trudy woke, and he went to her at once. He saw the pain in her face as she moved. He changed the dressing and applied more of the salve as she fell asleep again. Night had slipped into the hollow of the land when she woke and this time lifted her head.

"How are you?" Fargo asked.

"Better. That burning pain is gone," Trudy said. "How long have I been asleep?"

"Most of the day," he told her.

"I smell something delicious," she said.

"Dinner," he answered, and watched her push

herself half up. She winced but kept on until she was sitting cross-legged. The front of her shirt hung down from the collar still around her neck to somehow keep her properly covered. Fargo tested the bird and found it done. He cut off a piece and handed it to her. She ate gingerly but hungrily and sat up very straight to keep the front of her shirt in place. When they finished eating, Fargo cut the remaining meat from the bird and wrapped it in leaves. "It'll be good cold tomorrow," he said.

"I'll be able to go on tomorrow," Trudy said.

"Not likely," Fargo said.

"I'll be ready," she said firmly, her nose lifting skyward. She uncrossed her legs, stayed on her stomach, and crawled into her bedroll without allowing him even a glimpse of the side of one high breast. He went to her, put on another layer of the salve, and her hand reached out and closed around his wrist. "Stay next to me tonight. Please," she asked.

"Why not?" He shrugged and pulled his bedroll beside hers, undressed, and lay down. Her hand reached out, and she fell asleep with her fingers pressed around his arm. He lay awake and heard the cougar's scream rise into the night. Trudy woke at once, and he felt her fingers tighten on his arm. "He's gone into the hills. Go back to sleep," he said, and watched her put her head down again. He closed his eyes and let sleep come to him, certain she'd not be riding anyplace come morning.

When morning came, he rose, used his canteen to wash, and had just strapped on his gun belt when Trudy's voice called from her bedroll. "Clean off my back?" she asked, and he used the water from her canteen to cleanse the blood and dried ointment from her back. The wounds were clean, he saw, the angry redness gone from them, but they still had to hurt bad.

"You'd best rest more," he said to Trudy.

She pushed on the palms of her hands and sat up, still managing to keep the front of her shirt modestly against her. "What happens if I rest two more days?" she asked.

"We make up time. I'm due at Thief River come the end of the week," he said.

"That means losing two more whole days for me," she said.

"You were the one who went out cougar chasing, honey," Fargo snapped.

"I'll ride this morning," Trudy said, and pushed herself to her feet, her pert face set tight. She walked to her horse, pulled another shirt out of her saddlebag, and disappeared into the rocks with careful steps.

Fargo made a wry face. Grit as well as sass and fire, he noted, not without silent admiration. Trudy Keyser was a high-powered package of contrasts, little-girl eager sweetness and steely determination, quick-fire intelligence, and damn-fool stubbornness. And a truth she kept hidden inside herself.

He held her horse as she came from behind the rocks wearing a tan shirt, and he saw her wince as she climbed into the saddle. "Let's go back to the cougar tracks," Trudy said grimly. "Show me where I went wrong."

He shrugged and rode back to where he had followed her up the rock-lined passage. He halted just before the passage dropped off and dismounted. "Stay in the saddle. You can see from there," he said as she grimaced in pain. He knelt down and pointed to the cougar's pawprints. "Right here, he changed from walking to stalking, and you didn't pick that up.

See how these foreprints stretch out further? A stalking cougar tenses muscles, and his forelegs move out in long, careful motions. Not only that, he steps on paws tightened up, and the prints dig in deeper. Sometimes you can catch the point of a claw mark. That print over there has it." Trudy nodded, her eyes studying the things he pointed out to her. "You interrupted him stalking something, and he turned on you," Fargo said as he remounted and led the way back.

He headed north again, and she asked no favors as he set a fast pace. But he noticed the pain grow in her face, yet she continued to listen, observe, and learn. But when the day ended she slid into her bedroll in exhaustion after only nibbling at the remains of the grouse. "Please, next to me," she murmured, and he put his gear down beside her. Once again she slept with her hand on his arm.

When morning came, he watched her go into the brush to dress. She emerged with her pert face solemn.

"You hurting?" he asked.

"Not outside," she said with an edge, and he let the remark go unanswered. A silent grimness replaced the usual eager enthusiasm of her days as he worked with her, showing her how to take a horse sideways down a steep incline and making her practice racing through thick woods without slamming into trees. In the afternoon he slowed the pace northward and had her dismount often while he dug and pulled at roots and leaves.

"Trail food," he said. "Damn important if you're leading a train and the supplies run out and there's no game to bring down." He held up a handful of tuber growing on long root chains. "Groundnuts," he said. "The Pilgrims depended on these during those first winters when they landed. They're really tubers, but taste a little like turnips. You can pull them out of the ground by hand as I just did. Look for purplish-brown flowers, and the roots will be underneath."

"Cook them in boiling water with salt?" Trudy asked, and he nodded. He showed her how to find Jerusalem artichoke and the wild roots of burdock and spring beauty, the wild greens of strawberry spinach and lamb's quarters, wild cucumber and Indian lettuce. He taught her how to use the leaves and the roots of salsify and the tender leaves of green amaranth. When the day ended, she had taken in a lot, and he could see her mentally digesting everything as they sat before a tiny fire and finished the last of the grouse.

But when she went into the trees to change, her face had set itself tight again, he saw, and the silent withdrawal was around her like a cloak when she returned.

"There aren't many days left," Fargo remarked.

"I don't need to be reminded of that," Trudy said sharply.

"You going to spend the rest of them in that hole you're digging for yourself?" he asked.

"Maybe," she said. "Probably," she corrected.

"We made an agreement," Fargo said, pulling off his shirt as she sat atop her bedroll. "Two weeks to Thief River. You knew that was it."

"I didn't know a lot of other things then," Trudy said crossly.

"Such as?" Fargo asked.

"There'd be so much to learn," she said.

"Try again, Trudy," Fargo growled, and received a sharp glance.

"I didn't know you'd be saving my life or that you'd be what you are or that I'd want to stay with you so

53

much," she threw out in a stream of words. "There, does that satisfy you?"

"Makes me wonder something else," he answered.

"What?"

"If you feel that way, how come you keep staying in your own bedroll," he said.

"That'd only make it worse for me," she threw back.

"Maybe," he allowed. "But things are what they are. I have to go on. That hasn't changed any."

She held him with a long, almost sad gaze. "Things are what they are," she echoed, wrapping herself in her bedroll and turning her back on him.

He lay down and slept at once, unwilling to deal with any of the things she had said. When he woke with the morning, her arm was across his bedroll.

He woke her, rose, dressed, and rode out with her when she was ready. They were into the north country, and the nights turned cool with the hint of autumn in their caress. Trudy continued to grow grim, withdrawn, and yet she slept each night with one arm stretched out to touch him. She was becoming two persons, both fighting over something, both intriguing. But both could reach out to touch, one drawing sympathy, the other sparking admiration as she continued to absorb and gather in knowledge with acute sharpness.

It was late afternoon, and they had neared the edge of a long, narrow lake surrounded by white birch and three hills when he saw the near-naked horsemen, six of them threading their way down to the water. He grunted with a kind of pride when Trudy spotted them only seconds after he did.

"Assiniboin," he murmured as he took in the beaded armbands two of the braves wore. He swore softly. He and Trudy were in an open patch of hillside, and he saw the six Indians halt and gaze across at them. Unhurriedly, they turned their ponies and started to move toward them. "No more games, honey. No more tests," Fargo half-whispered to Trudy. "It's suddenly final-exam time."

"We separate," she muttered.

"Why?" he questioned.

"Splits their strength. Three are less powerful than six," she said.

"Good girl," Fargo said as he moved the Ovaro sideways into the trees, and saw the Assiniboin go into a trot. "You take the high ground, I'll take the low," he said, and caught the quick flash of her eyes.

"Thanks," she murmured, aware that the high ground would give her more cover. She pulled her rifle from its saddle holster and waited beside him a moment longer until the six bucks drew near. With a yell, she sent the horse racing up the hillside as Fargo cut to the right and headed down toward the lake. He glanced back to see three of the Indians peel off after him while the other three charged up the tree-covered hill.

He let the Ovaro go into long strides and quickly outdistanced the short-legged Indian ponies downhill. But when he reached the edge of the lake, he saw the three braves making up ground as their sturdy-legged ponies dug hard into the soft ground. He glanced back to see two of the Assiniboin stay on his tail while the third broke off to ride parallel along higher, firmer ground. They figured to make him shoot at two targets in two directions, he realized, while they concentrated fire on him. He caught the swishing sound of the first flight of arrows as they cleaved the air just over his head, and he leaned forward over the Ovaro's neck.

He had to turn their plans against them, make them

halt and become one target again. Another two arrows hurtled past, too close, and he yanked the reins hard and sent the horse plunging into the lake. He drew the Sharps from its case as the Ovaro raced into the water with an explosion of spray. When the bottom ground dropped away and the horse began to swim, Fargo slipped from its back, turned, and lay the rifle across the saddle. The first two Assiniboin had reined to a halt in surprise at the edge of the water as the third one raced down to join them. Fargo fired the rifle from across the saddle, and one of the bucks blew backward over the rump of his pony as though a great wind had sent him flying. The other tried to turn, but Fargo's second shot caught him full in the side. The Indian fell sideways, his arms wrapped around his pony's neck until he slowly slid to the ground as if he were just learning to dismount.

Fargo saw the third redman swerve his pony and race away along the lake as three shots resounded down from the hills. Fargo let himself tread water alongside the Ovaro as he guided the horse to the shore. Another shot sounded, and his lips pulled back. He'd taught her a lot and she had learned well, but learning and doing were two different things. He swore and slid onto the horse while still in the water and rode from the lake, racing for the hills. There were no more shots, and he slowed as he moved into the trees. The rustle of underbrush came to his left and he swung the Sharps around at once, his finger on the trigger. The rider came into sight through the trees, and he was surprised at the flood of relief that rushed through him. Relief and something else he understood for the first time: the pride a teacher feels in a pupil that excels.

"One ran. I got the other two," Trudy said, and couldn't hide the pride that came into her pert face.

"They chased me, and I ducked out of their sight for a moment. I jumped down and sent the mare rushing on. They went after the sound of the horse, and I got the two of them from the brush as they went past. I remembered, Fargo. I remembered and I did it."

"Go to the head of the class, honey," he said, and watched her smile. He turned and led the way alongside the lake up a wooded incline that led to a grassy plateau. A row of Canada balsams topped a low, distant ridge like so many green-uniformed sentinels in the fading light. He rode toward the ridge and halted halfway there as the darkness descended, pulling under a hackaberry to make camp. When he'd unsaddled the horses and laid out his gear, he paused under the branches of the big tree and his gaze peered at the still-distant line of balsams now touched by the moon. Trudy's voice cut into his thoughts.

"She lives past the ridge someplace," Trudy said.

He turned, met her eyes. The female intuition, he grunted to himself. It never ceased to amaze him no matter how often he saw it work. "Yes," he answered.

"You still going to visit with her?" Trudy asked carefully.

"Why wouldn't I?" Fargo returned.

"You're running late," she said.

"That's so," Fargo agreed, "but Thief River's only an hour or so past Alva, according to what she wrote a year ago."

Trudy's face darkened at once. "An hour or so," she repeated. "That means tomorrow will be the last day."

"Looks that way," Fargo said.

"I thought we'd have at least two more days," Trudy said, and looked away. When her eyes returned to him, he saw a parade of emotions that fought with each other—bitterness, warmth, despair, caring—and they all added up to pain. "You have to visit her, of course." Trudy sniffed.

"I told you about that when we started," Fargo reminded her.

"I'm tired of what you told me back then," Trudy flung at him. "It's all so convenient for you, dammit."

She started to spin around, but his hands shot out, closed around her shoulders, and pulled her back. "You listen here, girl," he growled. "You show up wanting me to teach you to become a trailsman. You come bringing me money and trouble, and now you expect I'm going to turn my world around for you. You change, and you want to forget about agreements. Well, it doesn't work that way, Trudy. Hiring's one thing. Owning's another." He let go of her, and she took a step backward, her face grown pale. He turned from her and took his bedroll down, laid it out, and threw another glance at her. "We'll work through midday and then go on. I'll find a spot for you to camp while I go on."

"Thank you so much," she snapped, and he let her sarcasm go unanswered. He undressed, and when she stepped from the other side of the tree ready for bed, she went into her bedroll without another word to him.

He slept quickly, annoyed at her demanding presumptions even as he felt sorry for that part of her that honestly hurt.

In the morning she worked with him and did well, as he had come to expect. The day passed quickly, and when he rode on north to the ridge, he found a good place to camp on the far side of the row of balsams. He guided the Ovaro into the place, dismounted, and surveyed the terrain. He decided the spot was far enough inside the balsams to be protected and yet afforded her a good view of the approaches.

"I can start you a fire," he said.

"I can start my own fires, thank you," Trudy said.

"Suit yourself." He shrugged and swung onto the pinto. He felt her simmering anger follow him as he rode down the slope and away from the trees. The afternoon slid down to an end as he rode a steady pace and found the double rocks Alva Brown had said marked the road to her place. He put the pinto into a fast trot on the narrow road, hardly more than a poor trail, and soon came in sight of the small ranch house just as dusk began to settle.

Alva had written over a year ago that she had a small pig farm, and he had expected something pretty run-down, seeing as how she never had any money after her pa died and pigs made most places run down. His brows lifted in surprise at the very neat, freshly painted, sturdy house and well-fenced pig sties that met his eyes. He rode to a halt, the door of the house flew open, and Alva raced out before he'd planted both feet on the ground, her arms flying around his neck.

"Fargo, oh, Fargo, what a surprise," she gasped out. "Damn, what a wonderful surprise."

He held her tight, feeling her narrow, trembling body, always a steel-wire package of emotion. He pulled back to look at her.

Alva had hardly changed at all, still small, with a slight, wiry figure, small breasts, and small torso with shapely legs in tight Levi's. Her face was still thin yet pretty. She had a straight nose, long black hair, and large brown eyes that held a constantly wide-eyed expression. She linked her arm in his and led him into the house.

"You look fine, Alva," he said. "Real fine."

59

"I'm glad for that," she said as he took in the interior of the house which was well-furnished with plain but sturdy chairs and tables and a maroon settee to one side of the living room. "Pig farming is doing well for you, Alva," Fargo commented. "From your last letter I didn't think it was."

"That was over a year ago," she reminded him, and he nodded in agreement. "I work hard, and I've had a few lucky contacts," Alva said as she drew him to the settee and sat down beside him, her fingers twining into his. "Why'd you pick this night to arrive, dammit?" she said with a half-pout.

"Something wrong with this night?" he asked.

"I'm expecting company tonight," Alva said. "This one night, wouldn't you know."

"The company of a gentleman friend, I take it." Fargo laughed.

"Not that kind of gentleman friend. A man who's sort of a silent partner," Alva said. "It's a long story I'll tell you about sometime, but he doesn't want it known he's in business with me. He can send me a lot of buyers, and it wouldn't look right if they knew he was my partner."

Fargo nodded slowly. "I can understand that," he said.

Alva's arms encircled his neck again. "You can come back, can't you, tomorrow night maybe?" she asked.

"I can't promise tomorrow night, but I'll find a time," Fargo said.

"Any night but Thursday," Alva said. "This is Thursday."

Fargo laughed. "We always had trouble finding the right nights, if you remember?" he said.

"Yes, but I remember most how great they were when we did," Alva Brown said, hugging him to her.

Her mouth reached up and found his, pressing, trembling, hard-sweetness that was Alva, her body becoming tense at once, her hands fluttering along the back of his neck. Her lips opened, and her tongue made tiny, darting motions. He heard her soft gasping breaths that brought memories rushing back from other times, other places, other years. The hunger in her pushed through her lips that moved against his and the soft, quick touch of her tongue, and she finally pulled back.

"I'd guess your visitor is strictly business." Fargo smiled slowly. "I know the taste of desire."

"You always did," Alva said, and rose. "You've time for a bourbon."

Fargo watched her get two glasses and the bottle, her little rear still as provocative as ever despite its thinness. Something in the way it wiggled, he decided, as if it were just waiting to be fondled. She sat beside him again, and they talked of old friends and old times, of things done and not done, and she rested her head on his chest.

"You've got to come back, Fargo. You can't just show up and vanish again," she said.

"I'll find a time," he said, and rose with her still clinging to him, the small breasts tiny pressures into his chest. "Your company's going to be showing up," he said.

"Yes," she said, disappointment in her voice. She went outside into the night with him, and he took her face in his big hands.

"I'm glad you're doing so well, Alva, real glad," he told her. "It's a nice surprise."

"Seeing you's a better one, Fargo," she said. "I'll be waiting every night now."

"Except Thursdays." He laughed.

She blew a kiss at him as he rode away, retracing

steps through the darkness under a three-quarter moon. He was filled with a good feeling for Alva and the way she looked that left no room for disappointment. Besides, he'd make sure to find time for another visit. He spurred the Ovaro forward, keeping a steady, ground-eating pace. He was finally riding up the slope toward the ridge when he caught the flicker of the firelight from the edge of the trees. He slowed as he neared, and walked the horse into the campsite. Trudy stepped from behind a tree, rifle in hand. He saw her frown of surprise as she stared at him.

"What are you doing back?" she asked as he slid from the saddle. "You didn't find her place?"

"I found it," he said.

"She wasn't there?"

"She was there," he said, and took down his gear.

He saw her regard him with sarcastic amusement. "Don't tell me the lady said no," Trudy slid at him.

"All kinds of reasons for saying no," Fargo answered as he lay out his bedroll. "Some good, some bad. Some happy, some sad."

"My goodness. I didn't know cracker-barrel wisdom could be so comforting," she said tartly as he began to undress, ignoring her malicious bitchiness. "It's really quite laughable," she went on. "You couldn't stay here with me. You had to see her. It was a commitment. All that sincerity for nothing. Or was it all just anticipation? But it doesn't really matter now, does it?"

He continued to say nothing as he lay down in his bedroll, stretched his arms up behind his head. Trudy stared into the fire, angered by his silence, her pert face set. He let another few minutes go by before he spoke.

"You won't make it," he said finally, evenly.

"Won't make what?" she retorted at once.

"Becoming a trailsman," Fargo said, a touch of weariness in his voice. 'A trailsman has to do more than read trails. A trailsman has to lead. That takes somebody who understands that there's more than one way and more than one level on which people know each other. It takes someone who can understand people. That means someone who's grown up. You don't fit."

"Damn you, Fargo. I'm grown up, a hell of a lot more than you know," she flung back.

"Guess I've just not seen any signs of it." He sighed and raised his head as he heard her get up. She strode toward him, anger in her face, dropped to her knees beside him, and fell across him. Her mouth sought his, her tongue pushed out angrily, deep.

"I'll show you signs," Fargo heard her mutter as she drew back and yanked open the buttons of her shirt, freeing her breasts to spill out with their own eagerness. Fargo took in their high firmness as they jutted forward, white roundness coming to red-nippled points centered on small, pink circles. Her breasts were as eager as she.

He pushed up onto his elbows as she undid her skirt and pulled it off, removing her pink bloomers as well. And Fargo saw her firm, compact figure emerge, her convex little belly, rounded hips, and small round pubic mound adorned with a very curly, very black nap. Her thighs were beautifully curved and firm. He opened his mouth as she pushed one breast forward, pressing the little red nipple deep into his mouth, the white mound following. He pulled hard, sucked in, and heard her cry. He pushed her onto her back, but she wriggled, pushed up, and he swung back to let her fall atop him.

Trudy's hands grasped his shoulders, fingers digging hard into his skin as she gave him first one breast and then the other, switching back and forth as he pulled on their soft firmness. He let his teeth gently bite down on the softness of the tip of one breast, and Trudy moaned softly, her round belly rubbing up and down against his pulsating organ.

"Oh," she moaned, and lifted her torso, and Fargo felt his seeking spear rise, pulsing, throbbing. Trudy's legs drew up, and she brought herself slowly down over him. Her cry had an edge of pain in its ecstasy as Trudy pushed her rear upward and brought herself down slowly on him again, then again, and her cries quickly became pure pleasure.

Trudy made love as she did everything else, he saw: aggressively, full of sass and fire, her fists pounding his chest as she came down on him again and again. She fell forward over him as she pumped and cried out. He felt her legs against his hips grow tight, felt her slow, suddenly pause atop him, press down, and take him deep inside her.

"Oh, oh, Fargo," Trudy gasped, her cries gathering strength, and she suddenly convulsed with uncontrollable spasms. She threw her head back and her cry was the crown of desire. Her head fell forward and she collapsed atop him but kept him inside her, legs clamped around him.

"I came, I came. Oh, Fargo," she murmured. "I never have . . . never."

"You haven't tried all that much, I'd wager," Fargo said to her.

Her round cheeks rested against his face. "Only once, and it wasn't good," she whispered. "Not like this. Take me again, Fargo. Now, now."

He turned, brought her over onto her back, and enjoyed the compact loveliness of her body, all of a rounded, firm youthfulness, a body that fairly burst with energy, the flesh echoing the pugnaciousness of the spirit. Her arms came up, circled his neck, and pulled his face down to her breasts. She moved her body sideways back and forth and rubbed her breasts over his face, letting him taste first one tip, then the other, then pressing their firm softness into him. Fargo's hand moved down over the round curves of her body, the little convexity of her belly, and pressed down over the curve of her pubic mound. He caressed her, his fingers moving through the tantalizing wiry softness of her very black triangle and down farther until he touched the warm wetness.

Trudy groaned, a surging sound, and he felt her push up, her portal seeking, flowing with welcome. She groaned again as he touched, stroked, caressed. But her passive enjoyment was only for moments as Trudy grasped out, pulled his hand against her, and began to pump up and down.

"More, more, deeper, deeper, Fargo," she cried out, and seemed to explode with energy as her torso rose and fell, her thighs clamped around him, fell away, and returned to clamp again. He swung himself atop her, felt the roundness of her little belly meet his hard-packed abdomen as she pushed herself against his every thrust. Her energy exploded in all directions, demanding to be matched, and Fargo felt his own passions respond as he drove furiously into her, his body an instrument of harsh gentleness, a contradiction of pleasures to reach that final pleasure.

Trudy's thighs continued to clasp around him and her fists pounded his back as she pumped, her driving energy surprising him, just as the quickness of her learning had. Her mouth sought his lips, and her kisses were devouring, echoes of the quivering contractions the temple of her body offered. When her hands flew open and dug into his shoulders, he was ready, and he exploded with her as she let out a spiraling, high-pitched cry that held only ecstasy this time, a hanging sound that sent the air quivering. He felt her legs squeezing his waist with astonishing force. As her scream spiraled away, she went limp beneath him, and only her arms stayed locked around his neck.

He drew from her slowly, and watched her stretch out beside her, marveling at how her round, compact body could still seem to pulsate with energy. She turned onto her stomach, and her round rear was beyond resisting, and he ran his hands across the smoothness of her.

"Was that grown-up enough for you?" she tossed at him.

"Enough." He smiled slowly, and her hands came up to cradle his face.

"Don't go on, Fargo. Stay with me. It'll be better than ever now," Trudy said.

"You know I can't, Trudy," he answered.

"You can, you can," she insisted. "I care about you. more than I ever thought possible. You have to believe that."

"I do, but that doesn't change anything," he said.

"I heard how students often fall in love with their teachers. I understand it now. You can't just ride out of my life. Forget about tracking some man you never even saw, somebody you don't care about and who means nothing to you."

"That's not it. I took a job. I'm going to do it. That's what I care about—my word," he told her.

"And I just walk away as if nothing's happened, as if tonight didn't happen," she said.

"No, you walk away with whatever it meant inside you," he said. "And with everything you've learned. That's what it was all about, wasn't it?"

"Yes, that's what I thought first, but it's different now," she said.

"Things don't always end the way they start," he said gently.

He saw a sadness take over her face, and she ran her hand across his forehead, brushing back a curl of his thick black hair. "You're one of a kind. I didn't plan it to end this way. It just happened. I can't help the way I feel," she said.

"Think of the good things. Don't make it harder on yourself than it has to be," Fargo said.

She put her head onto his chest. "You're right. Just hold me. I'm sleepy suddenly," she murmured.

"Wonder why," he grunted as she cradled herself against him. He listened to her as she quickly slept. He realized he was sorry it had to end, too, sorry he had the damn commitment. He was moved by her quick-minded, spitfire spunkiness. But he sure as hell wasn't going to tell her that. She'd race off with it as hope, and that'd do neither of them any good. He closed his eyes and slept. Trudy stayed cradled in his arms as if she'd been there often.

4

When morning came and he woke, he let himself enjoy the loveliness of her as she lay on her back, cone breasts pointing straight up, her round, compact body made of quiescent energy. Her beauty was not unlike that of a peach bursting with delicious firmness, he decided.

Her eyes opened, saw him watching her, and she came against him at once, all rounded smoothness. But he pulled her to her feet, and her face took on a half-pout.

When they rode from the campsite, she stayed beside him, wrapped in her own sadness and silence. He rode due north, and the course kept him well away from Alva's house. The sun was in the noon sky when Thief River came in sight as it flowed south toward Red Lake River. The town lay just beyond, and he rode slowly down the wide main street. Nothing special about it, he saw, yet it had pretensions at being more than it was. He saw weathered buildings bearing the names "Bank" and "Courthouse" and

"Town Hall," the signs more impressive than the structures they were on.

He shot a glance at Trudy and saw her round-cheeked, pert face held tight. "What are you going to do now? It's a long trip back alone," he said.

Her snub nose turned skyward. "I'll make it, what with all I've learned," she answered.

"Yes, I expect you will," he agreed.

"But I might just look for some work around here," Trudy said. "There might be wagons heading back, or west. First, though, I'll spend a day or two at that hotel in a real bed." Fargo followed her eyes and saw the white clapboard building with the sign over the entrance that read BOARDINGHOUSE AND HOTEL. Trudy turned to him, her brown eyes suddenly hungering. "You won't set out right away, will you?" she asked. "Stay the night with me."

"For another try at convincing me to go with you?" He smiled gently.

"For another night to remember," she said simply.

"I'll try," he said, and rode on as she crossed to the hotel. He walked the horse down the street until he came to the sheriff's office, the name lettered across a small window in peeling gold paint. He dismounted and opened the door, finding himself in a small office with two barred and empty cells directly behind the room. A man with a silver star pinned to his shirtfront looked up from behind a battered wooden desk. Fargo took in a prominent nose set in a heavy, tired face, salt-and-pepper hair, and eyes that held weariness in their faded blue orbs. "Sheriff Covey?" Fargo asked, and the man nodded. "I'm Skye Fargo."

The man's weary eyes widened, almost with relief, and he extended his hand without getting up. "Damn, I'm glad to see you. Been waiting on you," the sheriff said. "Sit down." Fargo pulled up a chair with a curved back and regarded Sheriff Covey's tired face. "It's been a bad week. Judge Little's been hounding me every day to see if you'd arrived," the sheriff said.

"The judge is anxious to find Jack Towers?" Fargo asked.

"Most folks are, but the judge especially so. Personal reasons on top of the official ones. The judge was good friends with both murdered people," the sheriff said.

"People Jack Towers murdered?" Fargo questioned, and Sheriff Covey's heavy face nodded with added grimness. "I got myself some information on Jack Towers. Tell me the rest," Fargo said, and settled back in the chair.

"He murdered Seth Owens, the town treasurer, and a few days later killed Seth's wife, Irma," the sheriff explained. "Judge Little and two other men came in on him as he was standing over Seth Owens. They grabbed him, and he kept yelling he was innocent. But Judge Little said there was no question he'd just done it. He even had Seth's gun in his hand. It seemed they were fighting for the gun and Towers won."

"Were you there?" Fargo asked.

"No, but the judge called me when Jack Towers got away as they were bringing him in," the man said. "I searched and couldn't find him. I never figured he'd go back to visit Irma, but he did and killed her too. He was seen running, and Irma was found in the yard outside the house."

"You know why he killed the town treasurer?" Fargo asked.

"Not actually, but I'd guess Seth caught him stealing money," the sheriff said. "Jack Towers worked for Seth, doing whatever chores Seth wanted done, ranch hand, courier, guard, whatever."

"What about the wife? Why'd he kill her?"

The sheriff threw his palms upward. "Can't say. I'd guess he was afraid she'd seen him kill Seth and he wanted to make sure she couldn't put his neck in a noose," the man said.

"Did Jack Towers have anybody working with him, any accomplices?" Fargo asked.

The sheriff's tired face screwed itself into a collection of weary lines. "Maybe. I don't know, but maybe. He's been spotted, so we know he's still hanging out in the general area. I've wondered if somebody is helping him. That's another thing that has Judge Little on edge. The judge is convinced Jack Towers is looking for a chance to come back and kill him. The judge was the first man to walk in on him at Seth's killing. He feels if Towers can eliminate him, he'll go off scot-free—no eyewitness, no one to accuse him, and no judge."

Fargo's lips pursed as he thought for a moment. It was possible. If Towers got rid of all the important figures against him, the chances were he'd go free. Yet it seemed the man was flirting with being killed or captured when he could just run. Any man could lose himself in the wild north country. He shook away musings and returned his attention to the sheriff. "I'm ready whenever you are," he said.

"I won't be going with you," Sheriff Covey said, and Fargo watched him pull himself to his feet by pushing hard on the edge of the desk. The sheriff shuffled forward, and Fargo looked down at the wooden splints that bound the bottom part of his leg. "Broke my ankle and my foot last week," the sheriff rasped. "Damn stupid accident. Had a farm wagon roll over me. I'm sending someone else with you."

"One of your men?" Fargo asked.

"I've got no men. I'm it around here. I'm sending a man named Frank Halloway," the sheriff said.

"He's no lawman?" Fargo said.

"He's a bounty-hunter by trade. But he's a lawman now. I deputized him on Judge Little's orders. The judge likes everything done legal and proper," Sheriff Covey said.

Fargo turned in his chair as he heard the door open and he saw the tall man step into the office. He was handsome in an authoritative way, silvered hair, a thin, angular face, a four-in-hand against a starched shirt over a dark-gray frock coat.

"Sorry, didn't mean to interrupt, Sheriff," the man said with a nod to Fargo.

"No, come in, Judge, glad you're here. This is Skye Fargo. Judge Harvey Little, Fargo."

Fargo rose, saw the judge's cool blue eyes brighten as he took the outstretched hand.

"Wonderful," Judge Little said. "I hope you can start first thing in the morning. I want that murderer brought in so I can try and hang him."

"If he can be found, I'll find him," Fargo said.

"Exactly why I had the sheriff send for you, Fargo," Judge Little said with crisp authority in his voice. "I'll be waiting for you when you get back."

He turned to the sheriff. "Have Halloway ready in the morning and keep one cell empty and ready," he said, turned on his heel, and strode from the office.

"A man used to giving orders," Fargo commented.

"Judge Harvey Little is the most powerful man in this town," the sheriff said. "He's not only the judge, he's the mayor as well, and he sees to it that every shopkeeper pays his tax, every rancher the property tax, every farmer a land tax. The judge says the money's going to be used to build a fine town someday."

"Sounds ambitious," Fargo said as he walked to the door. "I'll be here come sun up to meet Halloway."

Sheriff Covey agreed with a nod, and Fargo left and walked the Ovaro back to the hotel as night lowered itself over the town.

Trudy opened the room door cautiously at his knock and then pulled him against her. "I wasn't sure it'd be you," she said.

"I saw a dining room open next to the lobby. I'll buy you dinner," he said.

"I'd like that." She smiled and linked her arm in his. Her leg brushed against his as they walked, warm and promising. There was only another couple in the dining room as they ate, and Trudy had a bourbon with him.

"The sheriff tell you more about the man you're going to track?" Trudy asked.

"Some. It seems he killed two people. They want him so they can try him proper," Fargo told her.

"That sounds fair," Trudy said, and Fargo caught the edge of reserve in her tone.

"Sounds fair?" he questioned.

"*Being* fair doesn't always follow *sounding* fair," she said quickly and firmly.

"That's true enough," he admitted. "But let's talk about Trudy Keyser. Just how do you expect to pick up a wagon train?"

"Talk. Listen. Ask around," she said. "I'll find something." A little smile moved across her face, a mischievous edge in it. "I'll tell them I studied with the Trailsman. That'll make them take notice," she said.

"Might." He laughed.

She finished her bourbon as the meal ended and led him back to the plain room, an old double bed taking up most of it with only enough room for one chair and

73

a chipped dresser. Trudy turned and faced him. Her eyes were suddenly grave as she began to unbutton her shirt, fingers moving deftly. He started to undress quickly, the action becoming almost a race. He was rising for her instantly, and as the last bit of clothing fell from his powerful, hard-muscled body, he reached for Trudy and pulled her youthful, firm body to him. Her energy exploded as she all but leapt onto him, her legs coming up to curl around his hips.

He fell forward onto the bed with her, and her hands dug into his shoulders as she felt his organ pushing at her, warm and pulsing against her thighs. He moved forward into the welcoming entrance already made waiting with warm moistness.

"Ahhhh, Fargo . . . Fargo," Trudy cried out as he slid forward, the sweet friction causing sensations too intense to savor, wild enjoyment the only response permitted. He heard his own groan of pleasure as her compact body rose, pushed, pumped, fell back, and exploded under him with renewed intensity. As she cried out for more, he felt her lovemaking held a new dimension, more than desire, more than wild energy. There was a kind of desperation in her fervency, and when her thighs grew tight around him as the cry rose from her, he heard a thin edge of sadness inside the ecstasy of it.

Finally she lay beside him, half over his chest and turned on her stomach. He met her dark-brown orbs as she searched his face.

"Stay with me, Fargo," Trudy pleaded. "Forget the damn job. Stay and go away with me."

He smiled. "I thought this was going to be just for memories," he reminded her.

"It is, but I can't help asking. I can't help the way I feel," Trudy said.

"It was great. Keep it for memories," he said as he placed a finger against her lips.

Her arms encircled his neck, and she clung to him with surprising intensity, the firm breasts pushing hard against his chest.

"Fargo, Fargo," Trudy murmured. "Oh, my wonderful Fargo! Why can't things ever end right?"

He didn't answer, letting her cling to him until she finally relaxed her grip and turned to lie on her back beside him, her eyes closed. Without opening them, she turned, pressed her face into the crook of his arm, and went to sleep with the same desperate determination with which she'd made love.

When morning came, he slipped from the bed and used the big porcelain basin atop the dresser to wash. Trudy didn't move. She lay with her eyes tightly shut as he dressed. He smiled and let her feign sleep. It was best that way, he agreed silently, as he closed the door softly behind him.

Outside the hotel, he led the Ovaro down the street to where Sheriff Covey waited outside his office beside a big man wearing a faded tan stetson.

"Frank Halloway," Sheriff Covey introduced, and Fargo saw that the sheriff leaned on a cane.

Fargo felt Frank Halloway take his measure with eyes as gray as a winter sky. The man's face was a cold, tight-skinned mask, and he had a thin nose and bloodless lips that turned down at the corners. Fargo had seen faces like Halloway's before, on men who enjoyed pain and took pleasure in killing. Frank Halloway nodded coldly and pulled himself onto a big bay gelding.

"Let's get started," he said, his voice a flat, icy tone.

"Jack Towers was last spotted north in the Sun Lakes country," Sheriff Covey said to Fargo as he swung onto the Ovaro. "Luck to you both."

Fargo waved back and sent the Ovaro north out of town, setting a fast pace. Frank Halloway rode beside him in total silence. When they reached the Sun Lakes region, Fargo halted beside a stream to let the horses rest and drink. He watched Halloway check his gun, a Smith & Wesson seven-shot, rim-fire single action with ivory grips, a fast gun in the right hands. When he finished with his gun, Halloway gestured to a rise of high land topped by uneven rocky formations. "I say we go up there," he said.

"Why?" Fargo asked.

"Men on the run like rocky places. Makes 'em feel safe," Halloway said. "They look for them like a bear looks for honey."

"Not this one," Fargo said as he peered at a distant oval of blue in the midst of the countryside. "He'll be staying near water. We'll start with that lake up there."

Halloway regarded him for a moment but said nothing as Fargo mounted and started north again. Halloway was beside him when he reached the lake, which turned out to form almost a perfect oval. Fargo rode slowly around the entire lake, his eyes scanning every inch of its banks. He found plenty of tracks but none was the kind he sought. He set off again and found a small lake not more than an hour's distance away, this one shaped with irregular borders. Again he found prints—deer, elk, muskrat, beaver, and a half-dozen smaller animals—but no hoofprints. Halloway, he realized, missed nothing, his cold, winter-gray eyes taking in everything.

"Let's bed down here," Fargo said when he finished circling the lake and the night had begun to descend.

Halloway shrugged as he swung from the bay. "Good a place as any," he said. He took a strip of beef jerky from his saddlebag, sat down, and began to eat with a methodical, silent efficiency.

Fargo let him finish before he broke the silence. "The sheriff was lucky you were in town when he broke his foot," Fargo remarked.

"Covey had nothin' to do with it," Frank Halloway said. "Judge Little knew where to get me."

"Oh? You've done work for him before?" Fargo queried.

"Before he came here and since," Halloway said. "Judge Little's not a man you run away from easily."

"He tell you anything special about Jack Towers?" Fargo asked.

"Special?" Halloway asked.

"Anything that'd help us?" Fargo said.

"Nope," Halloway answered. "Just you find him, and I'll do the rest." He turned a cold glance at Fargo. "I just hope you're not wasting time searching all around these goddamn lakes. I don't like wasting time."

"I'm not," Fargo said, and Halloway's face reflected only cold skepticism. Fargo took down his bedroll and went to sleep, determined to find Jack Towers as quickly as he could. The less time he spent in Frank Halloway's company, the better. He slept soundly and woke with the new day and a plan already formed in his mind.

He'd make a wide circle, as though he were a huge lasso, encircling every lake, pond, spring, stream, and brook, and work inward from the outer perimeter of the circle. If he found nothing, he'd do the same in another area. The plan was thorough but painstakingly slow as he had to carefully examine every shoreline. He felt Halloway's irritation and impatience, but the man was a professional. He'd lay back and wait and give enough time until he was convinced to interfere. Fargo held a grim smile inside himself. It was like working with a rattlesnake peering over your shoulder.

They had traversed only the upper section of the imaginary circle when night fell, and Fargo was happy to sleep at once. The searching was slow and tense, and his eyes hurt from peering at every marking along every bank. But when dawn came, he led Halloway out again, this time down the left curve of the circle he'd drawn for himself. There were three ponds, a spring-fed well, and a small lake that bore the marks of unshod Indian ponies, but nothing else. The day had passed into late afternoon and he'd gone half through the bottom curve of his circle when he crested the top of a slope, Halloway beside him, and pulled to a sharp halt at the figure almost silhouetted beneath a black spruce.

The rider and horse moved forward, and Fargo's curse stayed under his breath as the afternoon sun glinted off short brown hair. He waited, his face hard as stone.

"Surprise," Trudy said as she halted, flicking a quick smile in Halloway's direction.

"What are you doing here?" Fargo growled through lips that hardly moved.

"I followed you. I decided to go along," Trudy said, meeting his stare with an even glance.

"You better decide different," Fargo said.

Halloway's voice cut into his barely contained fury. "Seems you know the little lady," the man said.

"I know her, goddammit," Fargo bit out.

"Aren't you going to introduce me?" Halloway said.

"Trudy Keyser . . . Frank Halloway," Fargo said tightly, and saw Trudy take in the man with her direct eyes.

"What happened to the sheriff?" Trudy asked.

"Broke his foot. I'm here in his place," Halloway answered.

Fargo saw him devour Trudy with cold hunger and Trudy meet the man's eyes with a casual boldness. She was trying to irritate him, he realized, and she was succeeding, which irritated him even further.

"You've got three minutes to ride the hell away from here," Fargo ordered, and she turned a calm, almost chiding glance at him.

"On the contrary. This will be a perfect way for me to learn more," she said. "I won't be in the way at all. I'll just ride along and watch."

"School's out, goddammit," Fargo shouted at her.

"I'm enrolling again," Trudy said, and turned her eyes to Halloway. "I'm sure Mr. Halloway won't mind if I tag along," she said sweetly.

"He sure as hell won't, honey," Halloway said, and Fargo saw the man's tongue come out to pass across his bloodless lips.

"I mind, dammit," Fargo threw at him. "This is my show."

"Bullshit, Fargo," Halloway snapped, his voice instantly ice. "You've got your job, I've got mine. You don't make any rules for me."

"She'll be trouble," Fargo said to the man.

"Nonsense," Trudy cut in. "I just want to watch and learn."

Fargo turned to her again. "This is no goddamn turkey shoot. We're looking for a killer, maybe with a partner."

"Then you might need nursing if something goes wrong," Trudy answered.

"She's right," Halloway injected.

"She's not riding with me, dammit," Fargo bit out.

"Then she can ride with me. I'll take care of the little lady," Halloway said protectively.

"Then it's settled," Trudy put in quickly as she tossed Halloway a grateful smile.

"Shit," Fargo rasped as he swung onto the Ovaro and sent the horse into a gallop, the fury churning inside him. He wanted to fan her round rear until she couldn't sit saddle for a week. She was like a disobedient, willful, spoiled child playing with fire, totally unaware how badly she could be hurt. She thought she had Halloway wrapped around her little finger.

"Damn-fool girl," Fargo swore aloud as he rode. "Headstrong, damn-fool little package."

Yet she managed to get her own damn way, he realized angrily, dragging him into looking out for her despite himself. He swore again and reined up beside a pond in the last light of the day. He scanned its banks on all sides and finally swung from the pinto as Halloway rode up with Trudy.

"Nothing," he grunted. "We'll camp here."

"I'll get us some firewood," Halloway said. "Trudy told me she likes her jerky warm."

The man walked away into a cluster of red cedar, and Fargo's hand shot out, grasped Trudy's arm, and spun her around to face him. "Take that smug look off your face. What the hell do you think you're doing?" he hissed at her.

"You wouldn't stay with me. I decided to stay with you," she said with instant pugnaciousness.

"You're making one big mistake playing cute with Halloway. He means to have your little ass for himself," Fargo said.

"Not everyone thinks the way you do. He's a sheriff's deputy. He wouldn't do that," she said.

"He's a bounty-hunter. Covey deputized him on orders," Fargo threw back, and Trudy's eyes narrowed. He watched her take in his words with more careful interest than surprise or alarm, and he frowned inwardly. Her reactions continued to be the unexpected.

"I'll be fine," she said quietly.

"Shit you will," Fargo growled, and turned from her as Halloway came back with an armful of kindling.

Trudy helped Halloway make a fire as night fell, and Fargo stayed off by himself during the meal and listened to Trudy chatter with Halloway, who said only enough to keep her talking. Later, Halloway's eyes stayed on her as she went behind the rocks to change, stayed on her as she returned and slipped into her bedroll.

Fargo's lips thinned as he undressed and folded himself into his own sleeping gear. Halloway watched her the way a broad-winged hawk watched a chicken in an open coop: confident he had only to wait the right moment to strike. Fargo swore again and closed his eyes. He was tired, and he let sleep sweep over him until he woke an hour before dawn to let arrested mind and refreshed body combine to think things over.

He knew one thing above all: he had to make things happen. Otherwise, it allowed Halloway to choose his time and place, and that was too dangerous. Fargo's gaze went to Trudy's sleeping form in the bedroll, and he felt a twinge of admiration. He hadn't been aware at all that she'd been following. She had learned well, no damn question about that much.

The sun began to spread a pink lace veil across the sky, and Fargo rose, dressed, and his eyes moved out over the north land. Jack Towers was still the first objective. The rest would somehow have to be fitted into that search. He put away his bedroll as Halloway and Trudy woke and dressed, then he gave the Ovaro a quick brushing and, when they were ready, led the way around the bottom of the circle he'd drawn for himself. Once again, it was slow, painstaking tracking, and Halloway and Trudy hung back some as he searched. He had come to the last lake of the circle, a narrow body of clear blue water when he spotted the hoofprints. His lips pulled back in a tight smile as he traced the prints a dozen yards back and then to the edge of the water again.

He was sitting quietly on the pinto as Halloway and Trudy rode to a halt. He gestured with his head at the tracks by the water's edge and met Halloway's hard-eyed glance.

"Could be somebody else," the man said.

"It's him," Fargo answered.

"How do you know?" Trudy cut in.

"These tracks come out of those cedars over there," Fargo said, pointing. "They stop, move, stop again, move again. The rider came slow, looked around every few steps. An ordinary man going to water his horse just rides up to a lake. This was a man afraid, a man who knew he was in danger."

Halloway nodded in acceptance, his winter-sky eyes narrowed. "How old do you figure the tracks?" he asked.

"Day, maybe two," Fargo said.

"No hurry, then. He'll be moving slow and careful. We'll catch up to him now that we've a fix on him," Halloway said.

"Can't say that for sure. He could be real tricky," Fargo answered, and saw Halloway's eyes fixed on Trudy's firm breasts as she took a deep breath.

He was willing to go slow because he wanted to find the time for something else first, Fargo muttered silently. It was time to move, time to pick Halloway's moment for him. He cast a glance skyward where the sun had begun to edge down to the horizon.

"You two stay here, just in case he comes back. I'm going to follow his tracks for as long as I can before dark. That way we can ride hard, come morning," Fargo said.

"Good idea," Halloway agreed quickly, only his cold mask of a face hiding his eagerness.

Fargo put the pinto into a trot and went into the line of cedars, but he slowed when he was out of sight. He guided the horse in a long sideways circle as he doubled back. He dismounted as he neared the edge of the cedars and the darkness crept over the lake. The glow of a small fire pinpointed the spot where Halloway waited with Trudy, and Fargo crept as close to the edge of the trees as he dared.

He could see the two figures beside the fire clearly. And as he watched, Halloway got up and walked to where Trudy sat with her knees drawn up.

"He'll be a while. It's time we got more friendly, sweetie," Fargo heard Halloway begin.

Trudy looked up. "We're friendly enough," she said.

Halloway halted beside her. "Not for me, little lady," he said, and reached down for her.

She used her left hand to bat his arm away, rolled, and came up on her feet with the Walker Colt in her hand and aimed at Halloway's abdomen. "Don't try it, Mr. Halloway," Trudy said, and Fargo could almost see her snub nose crinkled in determination.

Halloway shrugged and let a thin smile edge his bloodless lips. "If that's the way you feel, girlie," he said, and sank down in front of the fire almost at her feet.

"That's the way I feel," Trudy snapped.

"Whatever you say, little lady. No need to get all

mad about it," Halloway said calmly. "Didn't mean anything by it."

"Good," Trudy said, and Fargo shook his head as he saw her lower the gun. Halloway's move was quick, his hand by the fire flipping a burning piece of wood up and across the flames at her. Trudy's reaction was automatic as the burning twig came at her. She pulled back and turned her face away, and Halloway dived, landed half atop her before she could turn back. He knocked the gun from her hand with one blow and smashed a backhanded blow across her face. Trudy cried out in pain as she fell onto her back, and Halloway was on her at once, pinning her arms down.

"You come swinging your ass in front of me, you don't suddenly play hard to get, bitch," the man snarled, pressing one forearm against her throat while he tore her shirt open and pulled her breasts free. He ran his hands over their high, firm mounds. "There, now, that's better. That's real nice, real nice," Halloway chortled.

"Bastard," Trudy gasped as she tried to bring her knee up and around. But Halloway knocked it aside with his leg. With his free hand, he yanked her skirt and underclothes from her and pulled her legs free. His hand clamped down over Trudy's twisting pelvis, pressed hard through the black, dense triangle.

"No, no," Trudy cried out. She tried to twist away, but he had her in a firm grip. Halloway swung his body around, jammed one leg between her thighs, and pushed her limbs apart as he pulled the front of his Levi's open and his thick, heavy organ leapt free. Trudy screamed as it crashed down over her pubic mound, desperate fear curling in the sound.

"No. Don't, don't! Oh, no," she pleaded, but Halloway's grunting sounds drowned her cries.

Halloway moved higher up on her, dug his leg harder between her thighs, and she screamed in pain.

"You're goin' to like this, sweetie," he all but drooled, and Trudy screamed again.

Fargo rose into a crouch, the barrel of the big Colt in his hand. He waited another moment as Halloway fumbled in his wild eagerness, then moved forward out of the trees and crossed the few yards to the fire. He'd risked waiting. He wanted Trudy brought to her senses so that she'd be happy to leave once and for all. He ran now as Halloway's rear lifted, drew back, and he started to ram forward again.

"You're gonna give it to me, you little bitch," the man snarled.

Fargo, almost at him, suddenly stumbled, on a half-buried rock. He cursed as he went down on one knee and glimpsed Halloway's head turn, the man's eyes wide with surprise. Fargo recovered, ran forward as Halloway let himself half-topple from Trudy, trying to bring himself up. Fargo swung the butt of the Colt, and the blow sent the gun crashing high on the man's temple. But there was enough force in it, and Halloway toppled backward and lay still at the edge of the fire.

Fargo got to his feet as Trudy scooted backward, leapt up, her face chalk-white as she scooped up her clothes. She pulled bloomers and skirt on at once as Fargo stepped over Halloway's legs to face her.

"Get your horse," he said, and Trudy's face was tight. "Get out of here before he wakes up, and don't come back. This is it, Trudy. No more lessons, no more coming along, no more tricks, no more anything."

She drew a deep sigh, and he saw a terrible sadness come into her brown eyes. "No more anything," she echoed, staring at him for a long moment, then she walked to her horse. "No more anything," she murmured again as she swung onto the bay. She cast a last, long glance at him, moved the horse forward, and disappeared into the dark and the trees.

Fargo listened until the sound of the horse faded away, and turned as he heard the groan. He stepped back and watched Halloway sit up, blink, and pull himself to his feet. The man's winter-sky eyes bored into him.

"You shouldn't have done that, Fargo," Halloway said, each word sheathed in ice.

"You shouldn't have touched her," Fargo said.

"I do what I want," Halloway said.

"Same here," Fargo answered.

Halloway's eyes bored hard into him. "Only reason I don't blow your head off is that I need you to get Towers," the man said.

"I'll keep that in mind," Fargo returned.

"We'll settle when this is over," the man said.

"Whenever you want," Fargo said, turned his back on the man, and prepared for sleep, spreading his bedroll out on the other side of the fire. He lay down as Halloway took out his own gear and he still lay awake as the fire burned itself out. Trudy's pert face and suddenly sad eyes kept swimming into his thoughts. He felt sorry for her, but she had to learn that even stubbornness had its limits. Maybe, when it was all over, he'd meet up with her someplace. He'd like that, he admitted. She'd gotten to him more than most with her quick-minded learning and spunky sass. But first he had a man to track down, come morning. Everything else would wait. He closed his eyes and slept soundly.

Morning came in crisp but sun-filled, and he tracked the hoofprints away from the lake and through the cedars. Jack Towers had ridden with a slow but steady pace. He was careful, stopping often to check out the land ahead. But he was no trailwise fugitive, Fargo grunted as the tracks stayed in a straight line. Only when Towers crossed onto a wide expanse of thick grama grass did the trail vanish. Fargo halted and scanned the terrain on all sides until he caught sight of the sparkle of sunlight on cool blue water.

"That way," he said to Halloway.

"He was heading west into the hills," Halloway said. "Let's keep going until we pick up his tracks again."

"We won't. That way," Fargo said, and sent the Ovaro forward.

Halloway followed with a frown of disapproval, but Fargo rode on until he reached the lake to find a shallow, L-shaped body of water surrounded by sugar maples. He dismounted as Halloway rode up.

"You find any more tracks?" the man questioned.

"No. Didn't expect I would. But he'll come, after dark maybe," Fargo said. "I'll take this end of the lake. You take the other." There was no need to add more. Halloway would take proper cover. He was a professional hunter of men.

Fargo led the Ovaro into the maples as Halloway went on to the other end of the lake and disappeared into the trees. Fargo dismounted and sat down, his back against the gray, plated bark, at a spot deep enough in the trees that still allowed him to see across the length of the lake. He put his head back against the tree and settled down.

Time seemed hardly to move at all as he peered through the trees until suddenly he noticed the shadows were beginning to slide across the water. He watched their slow progress when he caught the movement of leaves at Halloway's end of the lake. He rose to his feet as he drew the Colt from its holster, his eyes focused on the distant trees. The branches moved again, and the horseman came into sight, moving slowly, carefully toward the lake. Fargo took in the rider. He was a young man with a clean-shaven, boyish face and sandy hair. It was a tired face with no hardness in it. That didn't mean much, he reminded himself. He'd seen enough baby-faced killers. He began to walk toward the edge of the trees, pulling the Ovaro along behind him as he watched the distant rider near the water.

Fargo halted as he saw Halloway storm out of the high brush on foot and felt the curse explode inside him. The damn fool was too soon, too eager, the man still in the saddle. But Halloway continued to charge forward.

"You're under arrest, Towers," Fargo heard him shout.

The young man looked back, dropped low over the horse's neck, and sent the mount racing along the edge of the lake. Halloway fired, but his shots went wild as Jack Towers lay flat over his horse. Fargo swore again, spun, and leapt onto the Ovaro and pulled the Sharps from its case. He raced from the trees, headed for the lake, and cut across the fleeing rider's path. Towers saw him, tried to rein up and change direction, but Fargo's shot plowed into the ground in front of him.

"You get the next one," Fargo called, the rifle at his shoulder, and Jack Towers pulled to a halt and sat quietly as Fargo moved up to him. Halloway had retrieved his horse and rode up from the other end of the lake. He yanked the younger man's gun from its holster.

"You won't be needing this anymore." Halloway laughed as he pushed the gun into his belt.

Fargo eyed Jack Towers carefully and saw that the brown eyes under the sandy hair held resignation, giving his young face almost a relieved weariness.

"Tired of running?" Fargo asked, and Jack Towers nodded. Fargo nodded to the lake. "You were going for water," he said, and saw surprise come into the man's eyes.

"You knew. That's how come you were waiting for me," Jack Towers said. "How'd you find out?"

"I do my homework," Fargo said. "Go on, fill your canteen."

"Thanks," Jack Towers said, and dropped from the horse. He drank thirstily before he filled his canteen, Fargo saw, and when he returned to his horse, Halloway moved closer to him.

"It's a long trip back," Halloway growled. "One wrong move and I kill you, understand, boy?" Jack Towers said nothing as he passed his eyes across Halloway. "You had somebody help you hide out?" Halloway asked.

"No," Towers said.

"I think you're lyin'," Halloway growled. Towers shrugged away his words. "I find out you are and I'll break your damn face," Halloway threatened.

"Let's ride," Fargo said, and turned the pinto south.

Jack Towers rode alongside him, Halloway following behind. The younger man rode in silence, and Fargo saw the weariness stay in his face as he led the way down a gentle slope from the lake.

"Why'd you do it?" Fargo asked. "Kill Owens and his wife?"

"I didn't," Towers said.

"Hah! That's what they all say," Halloway spit out.

Fargo realized there was more than enough truth in his words, but he made no comment as he guided the horse up and across a plateau grown thick with heavy brush, a thick stand of bitternut along one side. It was over, the rest only the task of bringing the prisoner in. It had ended more easily than he'd expected, yet he rode with his eyes scanning the land. Force of habit, partly, but also because he wasn't certain Towers had told the truth about being on his own. The day had started to wind to an end when they reached the edge of the dense stand of bitternut, and Halloway pulled to a halt.

"Camp here," he said as he dismounted. "He gets tied up for the night."

Fargo nodded agreement as he took in the deep woods that all but encircled the campsite Halloway had chosen. He peered into the already graying thickness of the woods for a long moment, saw nothing and heard nothing, and turned away. He sat down on a half-rotted log and watched Jack Towers fold himself cross-legged on the ground while Halloway sat down across from him.

"Eat before I tie you up, boy," Halloway ordered, and Towers pulled a stick of pemmican from his shirt pocket, bit off a piece, and chewed it slowly. But then there was no fast way to chew pemmican, Fargo reminded himself. He took out a piece of beef jerky for himself and stayed on the log as he ate.

The grayness of dusk had begun to spread when the gunfire exploded, not a single shot but a hail of bullets that slammed into tree trunks, plowed into the ground, and sent a shower of splinters from the log on which he sat. Fargo toppled backward over it, glimpsed Halloway diving for cover onto his stomach. As the Trailsman rolled behind the log, another volley of shots sent tiny geysers of dirt into the air. He heard the sound of a horse breaking into a gallop, lifted his head, and saw Jack Towers streaking into the trees.

"Goddamn," he heard Halloway shout as a third volley of shots slammed into the campsite.

"Shoot back. Cover me," Fargo said as he rolled into the brush, rose to a crouch, and raced for the Ovaro as Halloway fired wildly at the unseen gunman. Fargo vaulted into the saddle and sent the Ovaro racing into the dense woods. He heard Jack Towers to his left, racing through the bitternuts. Instead of losing time to swing over to follow in the fleeing prisoner's tracks, Fargo sent the Ovaro plunging forward through the gray woods. The gray would be replaced by stygian blackness all too soon, he knew, but he kept the Ovaro racing forward. He held the reins lightly, hardly guiding the horse, letting him use his own power and agility in his own way to swerve and race through the thick woods.

He raced parallel to Jack Towers, heard the sounds of the man at his left as the Ovaro gained on him. Fargo listened to the sounds of Towers' horse and heard the pounding of the horse's hooves as he swerved and turned, twisted and spun through the heavily forested terrain. Fargo guided the Ovaro left as well as forward as he decided he was abreast of the other horse. He let the Ovaro race on and the sounds of Towers' horse were close now, heavy sounds, the horse snorting hard, too many branches being snapped off.

The animal was tiring fast, brushing against too many trees, stumbling, having trouble with the thickness of the woods. Fargo had expected as much. It took an exceptionally agile, sturdy horse to maintain speed through thick woods and not crash into trees. He let the Ovaro slow some as he moved still farther left, edging closer to where Jack Towers tried to keep his horse moving. Towers heard him by now, he knew, and was helpless to do anything about it. Fargo, slightly ahead of the other horse now, swung still closer and came into sight of Jack Towers through the remaining gray light.

The man's horse was gulping too much air, snorting hard and laboring to avoid crashing into trees as he lost speed fast. Fargo swung closer and saw Towers peer over at him, as he kept the Ovaro paralleling the other horse. To his credit, Towers didn't push his horse until it dropped or smashed its brains out against a tree trunk as some men would have done. He sat the saddle as his horse continued to slow.

Fargo saw the tight-lipped resignation on Jack Towers' face as he knew exactly what had happened. His horse had been run down, as a wolf pack runs down its prey with simple stamina and agility. Towers pulled back on the reins and brought his horse to a halt, sat quietly as Fargo came through the trees, the Colt in his hand.

"We'll be walking back. We want your horse ready to ride, come morning," Fargo said quietly, and Jack Towers nodded.

He turned his horse and slowly began to walk the mount through the dense woods, Fargo behind him. The night came down to turn the woods into blackness, and Fargo listened for the slightest sound as he kept the Ovaro's nose almost on the rump of the other horse. Only slivers of moonlight drifted into the thick woods every so often as the silent procession moved slowly but steadily.

When they finally reached the campsite where the cleared area let the moon in, Halloway jumped to his feet, strode to Towers, and yanked him from the saddle. "Lyin' bastard," Halloway roared, and Fargo saw his arm come down, a chopping blow that sent Towers sprawling six feet away. Halloway was after him at once, yanked Towers up by the shirtfront, and shook him as a terrier shakes a rat. "Who is he, damn your lyin' hide? Who's workin' with you?" he shouted.

"Nobody," Towers said.

Halloway smashed him across the face with a backhanded blow. "Who, goddammit?" he snarled.

"Nobody," Towers answered, pain in his voice. "Nobody."

"Lyin' bastard," Halloway said, and hit him again. "Who?"

"Nobody," Towers said, gasped out the word.

Halloway started to raise his fist again as Fargo stepped in, gave Halloway a shoulder, and pulled Towers away from him. "That's enough," he said.

"Mind your own business. He lied to us," Halloway glared. "Somebody almost sprung him loose, and he's going to tell me."

"Not this way. You'll just beat him senseless," Fargo said.

"You're pushing me, Fargo. I don't like that," Halloway growled.

"I'll remember that," Fargo said, and reached down, pulled Towers up, and set him against the trunk of a wide tree. He left him there as the man used a kerchief to wipe blood from the corner of his mouth. Halloway sat down and anger continued to cloak him as he watched Fargo lean against a tree.

"We'd best stand guard tonight," Fargo said calmly.

"Goddamn right," Halloway muttered.

"Two-hour shifts so we can get some sleep too," Fargo said. He walked to the Ovaro and took his bedroll down, spread it along the edge of the campsite as he watched Jack Towers take a long drink from his canteen. When Halloway started to take his gear down, Fargo went over to where Jack Towers sat with his head across his arms. The man looked up at him.

"Thanks for stopping him," Towers said.

"Might not be able to next time unless you talk some," Fargo said.

"Nothing to talk about. Nobody's been helping me hide out," Towers said.

Fargo's glance was skeptical. "Somebody just tried to help you get away," he said. "You telling me that was Robin Hood?"

"I don't know who it was," Towers insisted.

"Try guessing," Fargo said, his voice hardening, aware Halloway was listening from his bedroll.

"I can't. I don't know," Towers said again.

Fargo's eyes narrowed as he searched Jack Towers' face and saw the man meet his eyes without wavering. "Why'd you stay here in the north country?" Fargo asked. "Why didn't you light out as fast and as far as you could get."

"I was trying to find Sam Delafeld," Towers said.

"Why?"

"He was with me when they said I killed Seth Owens. He can tell them I couldn't have done it," Towers said.

"Why didn't he?" Fargo questioned.

"Sam got scared and ran. He's been hiding out ever since."

"Why?" Fargo pressed.

"You've got to know Sam. He's afraid he'll be put back in jail. He's only been out six months. He's afraid they'll just say he was in on it and put him back too. Or hang him," Jack Towers explained. "But I've been trying to find him to talk him into coming back with me."

"What makes you think he'd do it if you found him?" Fargo asked.

"Sam owes me one. I saved him from a broken neck with a bad bronco once," Towers said.

Halloway's voice cut in. "Shit, that's it. He's tryin' to help you but stay out of it," he said, and strode closer. His eyes went to Fargo, waited.

"It fits," Fargo agreed.

Halloway leaned over Towers. "Your partner tries again, he won't have to worry about telling anybody anything about you, sonny," he rasped.

Towers stared away, a furrow on his brow, almost as though he didn't understand all that was happening.

"I'll take the first watch," Fargo said, and Halloway strode to his bedroll and lay down on it after tying Towers' wrists and ankles. Fargo settled back against a tree trunk a few feet back from the clearing where the moonlight didn't reach, and he let his ears become his eyes. The two hours were quiet, and when Halloway woke and took over, Fargo lay down on his bedroll and slept instantly. He woke and took up his second shift to see Jack Towers asleep propped up against the tree, and the night, broken up as it was, passed quickly. He led the way when morning came, and Halloway untied Towers so he could ride. Fargo set a slow pace as his gaze swept the land in front of them and on both sides, aware that Jack Towers watched him as he rode.

"He's gone by now," Towers said. "I know Sam. He's running to hide away again. He tried. He'll figure that's evened us up. He won't be back."

"That's what you'd sure as hell like us to think," Halloway snapped.

Fargo said nothing. Halloway's remark sounded logical and probable. But there was something about Jack

Towers that didn't add up to a hardened killer, Fargo mused as he watched the younger man ride beside him. Towers' words had cloaked no wheedling, no clever attempt to convince. They had held the resigned weariness of a man who had only his own beliefs left, a man who'd given up caring what others thought. But nonetheless, Fargo kept his gaze sweeping the land as they rode.

The noon sun hung in the sky when he turned southwest, and Halloway barked questions at once. "What're you doing, Fargo?" the man snapped.

"Staying away from that long line of hawthorns over there," Fargo said.

"You think he's in there?" Halloway queried.

"Maybe. If we stay away, he'll have to come out into the open to get close enough for shooting," Fargo said, and headed west as the line of trees curved west. He stayed clear of them, keeping to open land as much as possible, and the night began to move over the land when he turned into a rock-lined crest. He chose a spot to camp where tall rock formations formed stone walls on three sides of a small space. The day had gone slowly but quietly, yet Fargo still felt the jabbing uneasiness inside him. He dismounted and watched Halloway tie Towers again and sit the prisoner against one of the tall rock walls.

"Two-hour shifts, same as last night," Fargo said. "You take the first shift tonight."

As darkness descended and Halloway took up position across from Towers, Fargo pulled himself up onto the rocks where he found a long, vertical crevice deep enough for him to fit into. He let himself sleep quickly, woke when it was time for him to take up watch. He slid down, waited as Halloway stretched out on his own bedroll, and then climbed back into the crevice. The stone to his back and sides formed a perfect place for sound to bounce from and magnify as it did. He settled down and kept his breathing soft and steady. It wasn't long when the sounds of tiny claws echoed up to the crevice as wood rats and deer mice scurried on the rocks below. Down where the rocks ended, weasels and martens pushed their way through dry brush. But there was little else, the night still except for the distant sound of a coyote's howling.

The two hours of his shift were almost finished when the sound echoed up to him from the other side of the base of the rocks, faint yet unmistakable, the tap of a boot heel striking a protrusion of the rocks. Fargo straightened up in the crevice and listened. The silence seemed endless, but then it came again: a half-scrape, half-tap this time, someone moving very carefully across the rocks but unable to avoid a misstep in the dark. Fargo drew his Colt as he slid from the crevice. He could just see the dark shape of Jack Towers against the rocks below. The sound had come from directly behind him on the other side of the rocks. Fargo continued to lower himself down from the crevice when the silence was shattered by Halloway as he rose and strode from his bedroll.

"My shift," he called out.

"Shit," Fargo swore, and the sounds from the other side of the rocks were suddenly loud, heels half-sliding, half-running away over the stones. Halloway heard them now also, yanked his gun out as he ran out of the hollow and halted, peering futilely into the blackness of the night. He started forward; two shots rang out, and Halloway flung himself backward to land on his shoulders inside the hollow of rock.

"Go after him, dammit," Halloway shouted from where he lay.

Instead, Fargo slowly holstered the Colt. "Too late now. He's off and running," he said.

"Shit," Halloway said as he got to his feet.

"That's right, shit," Fargo said harshly. "You ever hear of waking up quietly? He was just about to come around those rocks. I would've had him."

"He got that close before you heard him?" Halloway frowned.

"That's right," Fargo said, and turned to Jack Towers. "Your friend is damn good," he said.

Towers stared back as he slowly shook his head. "I guess so," he murmured. "I guess so," and again Fargo saw only a kind of surprise hanging in the man's eyes.

"I'll stand my shift now," Halloway said.

"No need. He won't try again tonight. He'll figure we'll be ready and waiting," Fargo said.

"I'll stand my shift," Halloway said doggedly. "I'm taking no more chances."

"Suit yourself. I'm going to get a night's sleep," Fargo said, and went to his bedroll. He slept at once and woke only when the sun swept over his face. He rose, untied Towers, and let the man rub circulation back into his wrists and ankles as Halloway woke and put his gear together.

Fargo moved down from the rock formations as he led the way into the morning, continued to stay in open ground as much as possible. The sun came down hot and he saw Towers breathing hard by midday.

"You finish all the water in your canteen?" he asked, and the man nodded as he swallowed. "We'll stop at a lake," Fargo said.

"Hell we will," Halloway barked.

"He won't make it without water," Fargo said to him.

"I don't give a damn." Halloway shrugged.

"I do. I'm bringing him in alive," Fargo said. He pointed to a distant ribbon of blue against a hillside that rose up sharply behind it. "We'll stop there," he said, and saw Halloway's eyes frost with ice as he followed, his cold face expressionless.

The lake turned out to be almost an hour's ride and as they neared its shores, Halloway called a halt. "Get off the horse," he barked at Towers, who slid to the ground. Halloway met Fargo's questioning glance with contempt in his winter eyes. "I'm tyin' him up while he drinks. I'm takin' no more chances on him making a break. You can fill his damn canteen for him, seein' as how you're so concerned over him," he said.

It was only a half-dozen yards to the lake, and Fargo turned away. There was nothing to be gained by pushing Halloway too far yet. He walked with Halloway as the man led Towers to the edge of the lake and flung him to the ground.

"Go on, drink the way all the animals drink." He laughed, a snarling sound, and Fargo kept his silence again. The time wasn't right to call Halloway down. He wanted nothing more to get in the way of returning Jack Towers to the sheriff. His thoughts were still settling themselves when the shots exploded, and he saw Halloway dive to one side, yanking Towers along with him. Another two shots slammed into the ground, and Fargo flung himself into a line of brush.

The shots had come from halfway up the hillside where silver maple grew dense.

"Stay with him," he shouted to Halloway as he rose, ran in a crouch through the brush to the bottom of the hill, the big Colt in his hand. He glanced back to see Halloway start to rise and fall back as another shot whizzed over his head.

Fargo moved to the right as he ran up the hillside, stumbled on a loose twig, recovered, and ran on. He used the low branches to pull himself up with a swinging motion and slowed when the shots stopped. He halted, listened, but heard nothing, and went on until he'd reached halfway up the hill. He dropped to one knee, his lips pulled back in chagrin as he heard only silence.

He moved forward again, still in a crouch, and crossed the face of the hill at an angle now, his ears straining with each step. But he heard nothing, and he halted when he reached the center of the hillside and caught sight of the flattened bed of star moss where the gunman had waited. He'd been on foot, Fargo saw, footprints moving up the remainder of the hill. Fargo followed for a few yards and halted. The gunman had fled straight up and down the other side on foot. He'd almost certainly left a horse waiting on the other side of the hill. Fargo's brow furrowed and he knelt down to peer at the footprints. The heel on the right boot was chipped, maybe a quarter of an inch missing, he saw by the impression fresh in the soil. He tucked the fact into his mind and started down the hillside to the lake.

Halloway was standing over Towers when he reached the bottom of the hill, and the man flung words at him with icy fury. "The bastard tried again. He didn't figure his partner would be tied," Halloway said.

"Probably not," Fargo agreed.

"This is all for me," Halloway said, yanked the big Smith & Wesson from his holster, and spun on Towers. He raised the gun, brought it up to Jack Towers' temple.

"What the hell are you doing?" Fargo frowned.

"He's dead, his partner stops tryin' to blow us away," Halloway rasped.

"You're supposed to bring him in alive for trial," Fargo protested.

"I get paid whether I bring him in dead or alive. It'll be much easier this way," Halloway said, the gun still held almost to Towers' head.

"Sheriff Covey say that?" Fargo questioned.

"No, Judge Little did," Halloway said.

"He's going back alive," Fargo said.

"Screw that. I've had it with this shit. He's goin' back nice and dead, and I'm goin' to enjoy that," Halloway said, and Fargo heard him pull the hammer back on the pistol.

Fargo drew his Colt, and his voice grew ominously soft. "Pull that trigger and you'll go back the same way," he said.

Halloway turned to stare at him, surprise in the gray eyes. He frowned, his glance going to the Colt aimed at his chest. His own gun in his hand was still pointed at Jack Towers, and Fargo saw him measuring distances, gauging his chances. Slowly, Halloway lowered his arm as he decided Fargo's shot would get him before he could swing around to fire.

"Drop it," Fargo ordered, and saw protest flood the cold, winter eyes.

"You got your way. That's enough, isn't it?" Halloway said.

"Drop it," Fargo repeated.

"You can trust me," Halloway slid at him.

"I do. I trust you to kill him and me if you get the chance. You like killing, Halloway," Fargo said. "Now drop the goddamn gun."

Halloway's eyes were spears of fury as he let the

gun drop to the ground and stepped back. "You'll pay for this, Fargo," he said.

Fargo scooped the Smith & Wesson up and pushed it into his belt. "You get it back when he's in Sheriff Covey's jail," he said.

"You'd better start runnin' then," Halloway promised.

"Untie him so's he can ride," Fargo ordered as he went to the water and filled Jack Towers' canteen as Halloway freed the man. Fargo tossed Towers his canteen and swung onto the Ovaro. "You'll ride up ahead of me, Halloway," he said, and took a glance of pure venom from the man. "We'll ride south over the open land," he said, and fell back behind Halloway's big bay gelding.

Jack Towers rode alongside him and he felt the man's eyes on him. "Why?" Towers asked.

"Don't like to see a man shot in cold blood," Fargo told him.

"You saying you believe me?" Towers asked.

"Nope. I'm saying I was hired to bring you back to stand trial, and that's what I'm going to do, no more and no less," Fargo answered. "Now let's ride."

He set a faster pace for the remainder of the day, certain their attacker would need time to think through his next moves. If there were any. Maybe he'd given it his last try, Fargo pondered. He rode with his own thoughts and called a halt as the sun began to slide to the horizon and a long and wide stand of trees suddenly rose up directly ahead of them, mostly Canada balsam and Norway spruce.

"We camp here," he said, the land still open and a dozen or so yards from the first of the balsams. Anyone coming out of the trees would have to cross into the open long enough to be spotted.

Towers dismounted, weariness in his face, and Halloway quickly tied his wrists and ankles again.

"I'm sure going to enjoy seeing you dead, boy," Halloway said, pushing his face forward, almost touching the other man. "And I'm going to see to that. You can count on it," he added with a snarling laugh as he stepped back.

Fargo sat quietly in the last light of the day, his gaze on the balsams nearest where he'd made camp. Was Jack Towers' friend in the cool dark of the trees, waiting for another chance? or had he gone on? The thoughts moved lazily through Fargo's mind. Perhaps he had misjudged Jack Towers, he mused silently. Maybe the man was a much better actor than he seemed to be, his young face cloaking the devious depths of a killer. His lips pursed as he put the thought aside, a question still to be answered.

He rose to his feet as the darkness moved across the land. "No fire," he said to Halloway, and saw the man's eyes sneer at him.

"You goin' to tie me up, too?" Halloway asked.

"I'm thinking about it," Fargo answered.

Halloway's jaw dropped open in surprise. "Son of a bitch," he rasped.

"Some people you trust, some you don't," Fargo said evenly.

Halloway's eyes shot fury at him. "Mind if I eat first?" he almost snarled.

"Take your time," Fargo said as he took his bedroll from the pinto. He sat down on it, chewed a piece of beef jerky as the moon rose. The balsams and the spruce were quickly etched in silver as the moon rose higher, the land bathed in a soft paleness. His eyes went to the trees again. If the man was there, he'd be able to hear better than see, Fargo realized. The sound

of voices would easily carry through the night stillness to the trees.

Fargo rose and looked over at Halloway. "You finished?" he asked.

"Just let me get my bedroll," Halloway said.
"Might as well have somethin' soft to sleep on if I'm
goin' to be tied."

Fargo nodded, and Holloway walked to his horse,
took his gear down, and began to spread the bedroll
flat. The Trailsman took another moment to scan the
edge of the balsams, but nothing moved under the
moon's pale glow. Halloway was on his hands and
knees, tamping down the bedroll as Fargo walked
over to him. He had some lengths of rawhide in his
jacket pocket and he took them out as he knelt down.

"Wrists, first," Fargo said quietly.

"It's your show." Halloway shrugged and held out
one wrist. He began to bring his other arm out when
he suddenly sprang, sending his hand down in a
sharp arc. Fargo saw the rock in his grip, tried to duck
away, but the blow slammed into his forehead. He felt
himself fall. When he tried to get up, he peered
through a curtain of grayness. The rock smashed
down on him again, this time on the back of his neck,
and he felt himself fall forward. He shook his head,
fighting off the grayness that grew into black purple.
He felt Halloway yank the Smith & Wesson out of his
belt, tried to grab for the man with one arm, and was
sent sprawling, a sharp pain in his ribs.

"Bastard," Fargo breathed, heard his voice, shook
his head, and the purple seemed to lift, then turned
gray again. He forced himself to lift his head, felt his
palms pressed down on the soil.

"Dammit, dammit," he gasped out as the gray curtain stayed in place. He could hear Halloway's quick

steps, the man's voice a harsh shout made of triumph and pleasure.

"Him first. Then I'll see about you, big man," he heard Halloway rasp.

"No, don't, dammit. Not right . . . not right," Fargo heard his voice gasp out, sounding as though it came from some faraway place. He tried to lift his head again and felt his lips pull back with the pain of it.

"Say good night, sonny," he heard Halloway rasp.

"No," Fargo's voice cried out, a faint sound that was wiped away by the shot as it exploded and shattered the night. "Damn you, Halloway," he heard himself cry out, and there was despair and the pain of defeat in the sound of it. "Damn your rotten, stinking soul," he said and the gray curtain blocked out everything else.

5

Fargo lowered his head and snapped it sharply upward, ignoring the pain, and the curtain of gray shattered. He saw the ground, his hand, then a corner of the bedroll. He shook his head again and the remainder of the gray curtain shredded away. He lifted his head again, looked across the few yards, expecting to see Jack Towers' lifeless body lying on the ground. But Jack Towers sat upright, leaning back on his bound wrists, and Fargo blinked, his gaze focusing on Frank Halloway. The man lay facedown on the ground, a red stain seeping out from under him to slowly spread across the soil.

Fargo rose on one elbow as he drew his Colt. Disjointed answers flashed through his mind, instinctive realizations clicking off like framed pictures being shown to him one after the other. His eyes went to the trees, and he saw the dark shape moving into the open. He fired at once, not waiting to draw a bead, three shots sent hurtling across the flat ground, and he saw the stooped figure turn and race back into the trees. Fargo fired again and there was no answering shot. He lay still, strained his ears, and caught the sound of hoofbeats racing away through the woods.

Slowly, he pushed himself to this feet, reloaded the Colt as he walked over to Jack Towers. He stared at the man's chalk-white face, the terror still stark in his eyes.

"I saw death looking at me," Towers gasped, his voice a hoarse, raw sound.

"You did," Fargo agreed. "Sam Delafeld doesn't owe you anything anymore. He's paid up for sure."

"I don't understand it," Towers said. "I don't know what to say."

"Say a prayer," Fargo answered, and reached down, untied the man's bonds, and pushed the rawhide thongs into his pocket. "We'll move, find another place to camp," he said. "I'll send someone for Halloway when we get to town."

He climbed onto the Ovaro, waited for Towers to mount up, and moved into the edge of the balsams. He rode for perhaps an hour, found a glade just inside the trees, dismounted, and retied his prisoner. He lay down atop his bedroll, the Colt in one hand as he slept. But the rest of the night stayed quiet, as he was certain it would. He'd learned one thing about their pursuer: when an attempt failed to come off, he did not rush to try again but retreated to plan out another approach.

Fargo let himself sleep until the morning. Then he untied Towers and found a cluster of pear trees that provided breakfast. He rode on for perhaps another hour and called a halt in a glen of mountain maple.

"We'll spend the rest of the day here," he announced, and Towers frowned back. "We'll rest by day and travel by night. That'll make it a lot harder for your partner to sneak up on us."

Towers shrugged, the air of resignation still

clinging to his face. Fargo sat down against the red-brown bark of an aged maple and relaxed. There was no way to approach the glen by day without being seen or heard, the surrounding ground covered with small twigs that cracked like shots when stepped upon.

The Trailsman closed his eyes, let himself doze, woke when a herd of deer passed noisily nearby, then dozed again. When he finally woke fully rested, he stayed against the tree and let the afternoon slide toward an end. His thoughts drifted idly, a restlessness prodding their progress. He wanted only to get Jack Towers into Sheriff Covey's hands and turn to more pleasant pursuits. Alva Brown waited for him to visit her again, and maybe, somewhere, he'd catch up with Trudy. She had been the kind that stays with a man when all the passing bedmates faded from memory.

He snapped off idle thoughts as dusk swept down, and he welcomed the night that came in at its heels. "We're riding," he said as he untied Towers again and led the way through the forest of balsam and spruce, the ground a soft, almost trackless bed. He set a fast pace and was convinced Sam Delafeld would follow, but he'd have to wait till day to pick up any kind of trail, and following it would take time and energy. The forest came to an end, and Fargo led the way into brush-covered hill country, kept the pace until dawn streaked the sky with ribbons of pink.

He found a rock overhang that went back deep enough to offer shade from the sun and a hiding place from prying eyes. He bound Jack Towers after the man finished his pemmican.

"Get some sleep," he said. "We'll stay here till night. If your partner manages to pick up our trail, it's damn unlikely he'll reach here till after dark, and we'll be gone by then."

He turned from the man, pulled his bedroll from the Ovaro, and squinted out across the terrain in the last of the night. A long cluster of box elder lay some hundred yards down from the overhang, and high brush covered the rest of the nearby land. Satisfied, he lay down and slept at once. He stayed asleep, drawing renewed energy back into his tired body until the cool wind of dusk against his face woke him.

He rose, saw Towers come awake, and untied the man. Chewing on a piece of beef jerky, Fargo stepped to the edge of the overhang as dusk gathered itself. He looked down at the land they had traveled during the night. He gazed across the low hills, slowly scanned the land, and brought his eyes down to the cluster of box elder. He stared at the trees as he felt the frown dig into his brow first, then the surge of almost disbelief that followed. The branches of the trees swayed, moved in that slow, straight line, the unmistakable movement that meant only one thing: someone made his way carefully through the trees.

"I'll be dammed," Fargo said softly.

He continued to stare down at the box elders. No ordinary horseman pushing his way through the trees, he grunted. The branches would be shaking harder, the line of movement quicker. This rider traveled slowly, carefully, and Fargo felt the surprise jab at him again. He had underestimated the man. Sam Delafeld showed both trail skill and a doggedness that made it too dangerous to let him stay the hunter. The hunter always held the options. It was time to change that, to put an end to the pursuit he thought he'd turned away twice already.

He barked orders at Towers. "Let's ride," he said, and moved out from the rock ledge, Towers beside him. He rode boldly into the open, the dusk still affording enough light to see a good distance, confident that their pursuer saw them leave. He rode toward a distant hillside that wore a thick cover of spreading white walnut, not hurrying his pace, and the night came down before he reached the hill. When he drew up to its base, he rode a dozen yards farther up the start of the slope before he halted.

"We'll camp here for the night," he said, and drew a frown of surprise from Towers. "Change of plans," he said nonchalantly. "Going to make us a fire, too."

Towers continued to frown as he watched Fargo pull together a pyramid of small twigs and light the fire. "I've been sleeping all day," Towers said. "I can't sleep more now."

"You will. A little extra sleep is good for you," Fargo said. "Over there," he ordered, and gestured to the wide trunk of a tree at the very edge of the firelight's circle.

Towers sat down against the tree, and Fargo bound his hands and feet again. When he finished, he took his own bedroll from the Ovaro and put it down at the other side of the fire, where it was half in shadow as the flickering flames already began to burn down the dry pieces of wood. He gathered a few handfuls of leaves and pushed them into the bedroll to give it form and lay down against it. He lay still and let the fire burn down until he and the bedroll were outside the direct circle of its glow. He let it burn down another ten minutes until it was a small center of flame and slowly began to inch sideways in the darkness. He continued to inch himself along the ground until he was in the deep darkness of the woods, and the bedroll in the shadowed glow seemed to hold a sleeping form.

He rose to his feet and began to climb, moving

along the hillside in a right to left circle. The moon rose high enough to begin to filter through the tree cover, and the woods became a dappled pattern of silver light and dark shadow. He crept forward, testing each step before putting his foot down firmly, and moved through the trees with the silence of a stalking mountain lion. Below, he could see the tiny glimmer of flame. He finally dropped to one knee beside a gray-barked tree trunk and began to listen. He had come up the hill far enough, he estimated, made the circle long enough.

Now it was time to let his trained hearing sort out the night sounds. He stayed silent, hardly breathing, and drew in the clicking of beetles, the soft humming of dragonflies, the sudden swish of air made only by bats as they swooped, the quick scurrying noise of deer mice, and then, suddenly, the sound he was waiting to hear. The footsteps were a faint, shuffling sound, steps carefully being slid along the ground. A grim smile touched his lips. The man was good, but not that good. His steps inched along carefully, but the faint shuffling sound stayed. A mistake, Fargo grunted silently. His feet should come down flat with each step. Flat ensured silence.

He peered through the trees as the sound drew closer, and suddenly the figure appeared, crouched low, moving downward toward the flickering fire-light at the base of the hill. He let the figure go on before he rose, the Colt in his hand, and swung behind on flat, silent steps. The figure moved through an open patch of pale silver light, and Fargo followed, dropping to one knee as he reached the spot. He peered at the footprint and saw the chipped mark of the right heel. He rose, followed, waited for the crouched figure to step into another patch of moonlight.

"That's far enough," he called out. "Don't move." He saw the figure halt, freeze in place. "Now turn around real slow," he ordered as he moved down the slope in one long-legged stride. He halted, Colt raised, and saw short brown hair swing as the figure straightened up and turned, looked at him out of a pert, snub-nosed face. He felt his mouth drop open, heard the gasp of breath escape him, and he stared until he finally found his voice. "Goddamn," he breathed. "You?" Trudy glowered back at him in silence. "Give me the Walker," he said. "Nice and slow."

She took the gun from its holster and handed it butt-first to him, and the frown dug deep into his brow as he stared at her.

"What the hell are you doing?" he asked, his voice rising as the anger surged through him. "Is this some kind of damn game for you? More trying to prove yourself?"

Her face lifted, met his angry glare. "No games. No proving," she said.

"Then what, dammit?" Fargo flung at her.

"Jack Towers is my brother," she said.

He knew his mouth still hung open as her words crashed against his sense of disbelief. "Say that again," he finally asked.

"Jack Towers is my brother," she repeated evenly, her lips tight. He peered hard at her and found truculence could be a mask.

"Start down the hill," Fargo ordered harshly. "I don't know what to believe about you anymore."

She turned and began to hurry down the slope ahead of him, but he was at her heels as she reached the bottom and stepped into the dim glow of the fire. His eyes were riveted on Jack Towers, and he saw the man look up, his eyes grow wide and shocked surprise flood his young face.

"Sis!" Jack Towers gasped out. He tried to get up but fell back, and Trudy ran to him, dropped to her knees beside him.

"Jack, oh, Jack," she cried out as she wrapped arms around him.

"I'll be a wall-eyed lizard," Fargo muttered as he watched.

"What are you doing here, Trudy? How'd you find me?" Jack Towers asked his sister.

"She had a damn guide," Fargo cut in, bitter anger in his voice. Trudy pushed to her feet and turned to face the blue ice of his eyes. "Goddamn, you had me teaching you how to hunt me down," Fargo bit out as anger pushed through the sense of disbelief that still clung to him.

"No, how to save my brother," Trudy corrected him.

"No wonder you worked so hard to keep me from going on," Fargo said, riding roughshod over her reply. " 'Stay with me. I care,' " he mimicked. "All that talk about falling in love with your teacher. Bullshit, all of it. You put on a hell of an act, honey."

"That part wasn't an act," she said, her pert face solemn.

Bitterness curled in his harsh laugh. "You don't think I'm going to believe a damn thing you say now, do you?" he charged.

"No, but it's true, whether you believe it or not," Trudy said, her pugnaciousness flaring at once. "There's something else. I'll remind you that Jack would be a dead man now if it wasn't for me."

Fargo's lips pressed hard into each other. "I'll give you that," he conceded. "But if you'd stayed out of it, Halloway would've just brought him back with me."

"Maybe and maybe not," Trudy said doggedly.

"We'll never know that," Fargo told her.

"No, but I know one thing: Jack didn't kill anybody. He's innocent. He couldn't murder. It's not in him."

"Then he can prove it to the judge," Fargo said.

"Only I can't. I'm being railroaded," Jack Towers broke in. "And Sam Delafeld's still hiding someplace. I knew it wasn't Sam coming after us. It just wasn't his way, but I never thought of Trudy." His eyes went to his sister. "News travels, I guess," he said.

"Yes, and when I heard about it I knew it had to be all wrong. I knew I had to come and get you free," Trudy said. "I asked a lot of questions, found out what had happened."

"And decided to play me for a fool," Fargo said. "Did a damn good job of it, too, I'll admit that."

"I didn't play you for a fool. I didn't do it for that," she protested quickly.

"Comes out the same way." Fargo shrugged.

"And I didn't lie about the caring. I didn't expect that would happen. It wasn't just to keep you from going after Jack," she insisted.

"Just a big coincidence," Fargo said.

"Yes, if that's what you want to call it," Trudy snapped. "You don't want to believe me. It might make you understand."

"I understand you gave me one hell of a fast shuffle, honey," Fargo said, turning aside her protests.

Her snub nose turned upward. "I did what I had to do. Isn't that what you always say?" she returned tartly.

"And it's what I'm going to say now," he answered as he strode to the Ovaro and cut a length of rope from the loop hanging down from the lariat strap. He started toward her as she frowned.

"Are you really going to tie me?" she said.

"You're damn right I am," Fargo bit out as he bound her hands behind her back and her ankles together. He sat her down beside her brother when he finished. "You had a horse," he said.

"At the other edge of the hill," she glowered.

"We'll pick him up in the morning," he answered and went to his bedroll at the other side of the fire, which had all but burned itself out. He lay down and felt the seething anger keep him awake as Trudy and her brother talked in hushed tones. He didn't give a damn, he grunted angrily. They could make plans, hold family reminiscences or whatever. It didn't matter. Jack Towers was going back and Trudy with him.

Fargo felt the surge of bitter anger as he thought about her. She'd learned everything he had taught her so she could use it against him. Damn her devious little hide, he swore. Worst of all, he couldn't deny the grudging admiration for her that kept jabbing at him, for her quick learning, for her unswerving determination, for the sass and spunk with which she carried it through. He didn't really disbelieve her about the caring. He remembered the pain in her eyes and the desperation in her lovemaking. They were real. But it hadn't stopped her from what she'd set out to do, and he could only admire her for that. Damn, he grunted again as he turned on his side and pulled sleep around himself.

When morning came, Fargo untied Trudy first and received a sleep-filled glower, and then her brother. Jack Towers had a new air of hope in him, the resigned weariness all but gone from his face. Skye waited till everyone had washed and dressed and breakfasted on a nearby mulberry bush before he climbed into the saddle, and he swept both Trudy and her brother with a hard gaze.

"You'd best understand something right now," he said. "One wrong move by anybody, and you stay tied all the way back."

Jack Towers nodded, and Fargo's eyes waited on Trudy.

"If you'll hear Jack out, listen to his side of it," she said.

Fargo shrugged. "It's a long ride, I can't help but listen," he said. "Let's get your horse first." He swung in behind Trudy and her brother as she led the way to her bay and climbed onto the mount. Fargo let her and her brother ride together as he rode a dozen feet away from the pair and led the way south once again across gently rolling land dotted with lakes and timber. Trudy edged her horse over toward his, and he met her direct brown eyes as they searched his face.

"Jack told me all of it last night. Will you listen to him now?" she asked.

Fargo looked across at Jack Towers. "Talk," he grunted.

The younger man drew a deep breath. "I didn't kill anybody," he said. "I was trapped. It was planned so it'd look like I killed Seth Owens."

"Who planned it?" Fargo queried.

"I don't know that, but somebody did," Jack Towers said.

"You were working for Seth Owens, right?" Fargo asked.

"That's right," Towers said.

"Word has it that he caught you stealing money and that's why you killed him," Fargo said.

"Word has it all wrong. It's a lie," Jack Towers said.

"I was told you were caught with the gun in your hand, Seth Owens' gun," Fargo prodded. "You were fighting for it when you shot him."

"I had the gun in my hand because I picked it up when I found him," Towers said. "I came to his house in the morning as usual, went inside, and found him dead on the floor, shot through the head. I picked up his gun to see if it had been fired when they burst in on me."

"Who?"

"Judge Little and two men," Towers said. "I say they had to be waiting for me. They knew I usually came to Seth's house in the morning."

"You saying Judge Little set you up?" Fargo frowned.

"I can't say that for sure but he wouldn't listen to a damn thing I said and he was awful quick to pin it on me," Towers answered.

"A man believes what he sees, usually," Fargo said. "I was told he was there to keep an appointment with Seth Owens when he walked in on you."

"If it wasn't him, it was somebody else, somebody who knew when I always got to Seth's house and knew the judge was going to be there," Towers said. "But I know it was planned to make me the killer. I guessed Seth Owens had been killed hours before I got there, when I was with Sam Delafeld. That's why I've been trying to find Sam. He could tell them we were together all that night."

"Seems like he's not much interested in telling anybody anything," Fargo commented.

"I told you, Sam's afraid he'll be dragged in, afraid they won't listen to a man just out of jail six months. Mostly he's just plain afraid," Jack Towers said.

"Why didn't you tell them you had somebody who could prove you didn't do it?" Fargo asked.

"I did, but they only laughed. When I saw they weren't about to listen to a damn thing I said, I ran, broke away when they started to bring me in," the man replied.

"What about Irma Owens? Word is you were seen running away from her body outside the house," Fargo speared.

"That's right," Towers admitted, and Fargo felt a stab of surprise. "I went back to the house a day or two later to talk to Irma. She always liked me. I was sure she'd know I didn't kill Seth, and I wanted to find out where she was that morning."

"You find out?" Fargo questioned.

"Yes, she'd spent the night at her sister's place. I also found out she was real afraid of something. I told her I'd take her someplace to hide and where we could talk. She agreed. She wanted to get away real bad. She went outside with me and somebody shot her from behind the trees, shot her dead right in front of me. I ran like hell," Jack Towers said.

"Somebody saw you running," Fargo put in.

"More'n likely. I remember seeing a sulky passing, but I just wanted to get away from there. Of course, they said I'd killed Irma too, and I guess it looked like that. Only I didn't, dammit, I didn't," Jack Towers said angrily.

Fargo rode in silence for a spell, his eyes narrowed in thought as he weighed Jack Towers' explanations against Sheriff Covey's account of the two shootings. It was like looking at the same picture painted by two different artists. The same things were in each picture, but everything was drawn in differently, everything a different color.

Trudy's voice cut into his thoughts. "You've heard it now. Jack's being railroaded, made to pay for something he didn't do," she said righteously.

"Hearing isn't knowing," Fargo said.

"You mean you won't believe him," she snapped, instantly angry.

"I mean it's not for me to believe or not to believe," Fargo said. "That's for others to decide. My job is to bring him in to stand trail."

"You're helping to let an innocent man be railroaded into a hangman's noose."

"And you want me to take words as proof. I can't, no matter how good they sound to you," Fargo shot back.

"You won't let yourself believe Jack. It's simpler for you this way, no questions to ask yourself, no conscience to face. Just do your job and the hell with right and wrong," Trudy flung at him.

"And you won't let yourself not believe. It's easier for you this way, no chance to wrestle with faith, no ugly places to face. Just keep believing and the hell with maybe being wrong," he returned.

Trudy turned away, but he saw her lips quiver before they tightened down on each other. He felt the anger simmer inside her as she moved her horse forward. She believed too much to allow for anything less, on anyone's part, and as she rode, she edged her horse toward her brother, almost as a gesture of withdrawal.

Fargo maintained an unhurried pace, stopped at a lake to let Jack Towers refill his canteen, and when night came, he made camp in land open enough to see in all directions nearby. They ate in silence, without a fire, and when they'd finished, he went to Jack Towers first with the rawhide thongs.

"Is this necessary?" Trudy asked with a mixture of annoyance and disdain as as he approached her.

"Makes me sleep better," Fargo said.

"What if I promised I woudn't try to get away?" she asked.

"Wouldn't change anything," Fargo said, and saw her eyes take on instant fire.

"Bastard," she snapped.

"Temper, temper," Fargo answered as he began to tie her wrists.

"It's nice to know what you really think of me," Trudy said, and managed to sound hurt.

"You've a bad memory. I told you that when we first met," Fargo said. "You're full of sass and spunk, and you go after what you want. You'd fight, even kill."

"Oh, yes, but I wouldn't cheat," she said.

"That's right," he replied affably.

"Forgive me if I don't say thank you." She sniffed.

"Sure," he said while he tied her ankles.

"I'm sorry I ever let you make love to me," she said, lowering her voice so only he could hear.

"No, you're not." Fargo smiled. "You're only sorry it didn't do all you wanted. Now get some sleep." He helped her sit down near her brother and went back to his own bedroll, where he closed his eyes and let the night quickly pass into dawn.

When Fargo woke, he heard Trudy talking to Jack Towers in whispered tones. She stopped when he rose, and he washed and dressed beside the stream and had the distinct feeling of trouble ahead. The feeling stayed as he untied Trudy and her brother and let them wash and breakfast. He wrestled with the thought of keeping their hands tied while they rode, and only the sadness in Trudy's eyes as she glanced at him made him decide against it. But misgivings stayed curled inside him as he mounted the Ovaro.

"How'd you get to be Trudy Keyser?" he asked her.

"My mother's maiden name," she answered crossly. "I've never been married, if that's what you're thinking."

"I'm sure of that," he said, and drew a frigid stare. He moved forward and Trudy fell into place beside her brother. Fargo set an unhurried but steady pace until he halted at noon to rest the horses.

"What are you going to tell them about me?" Trudy asked him.

"Haven't decided about that yet," Fargo answered, and she took the reply in silence.

When they rode on into the afternoon, the land grew into sycamore-covered hills with heavy underbrush. Fargo paused and his eyes narrowed as he surveyed the terrain. To go around the hills would add another day and he swore silently. He shot a glance at Jack Towers and Trudy as they sat side by side on their mounts, and decided to go on. Towers had too much common sense to try anything, and Trudy wouldn't go without him. Fargo moved the Ovaro forward and started up the first of the low hills by midafternoon.

He moved slowly through knee-high brush and noted that Trudy kept between him and her brother. Her quick glances and half-whispered asides to Jack Towers grew more frequent, and Fargo kept his face immobile as he grimaced inwardly. She was planning to make a move, probably a run for it, he decided. But this was the wrong terrain for it, he grunted silently, the underbrush too heavy for speed and too thick for silence. She had forgotten the things he had taught her, it seemed, and he felt a real stab of disappointment. He'd thought she'd do better, he told himself.

He rode on down the other side of the low hill, and the underbrush remained heavy. In the distance, he spotted the blue strip of a wide stream where the brush and tree cover began to thin. But that was a good distance away and the afternoon had begun to slide to an end. A pair of heavy, brown-barked sycamores leaned toward each other to narrow the pathway, and Fargo moved his horse closer to Trudy. He slowed, gestured for her to swing in front of him when she turned in the saddle. She took him by surprise by diving directly at him from her horse.

"Now," she cried out as she slammed into him, wrapping both arms around him as he saw Jack Towers swerve to the right and send his horse into the trees at a full gallop.

Trudy clung, her arms tight around him and she drew her knees up to try to wrap her legs around his.

"Let go, Trudy. Don't be stupid," Fargo growled as he heard Jack racing through the brush.

"No, damn you," she hissed.

His lips drew back in irritation more than anger. "Goddammit, Trudy," he snapped as he pushed his powerful arms outward with a sudden, sharp motion. Her grip broke, and she slid down along the side of the horse, hit the ground, and fell onto her round little rear. "Little fool," he flung at her as he sent the Ovaro racing away and glimpsed her glower as she looked up at him from the ground.

He plunged the horse into the heavy underbrush and cursed as the noise made it impossible for him to hear the sound of Jack Towers racing on ahead. He had to follow the fleeing horse and rider by the path of crushed and broken underbrush, and he swung onto the trail to see that Towers had raced on in almost a straight line. The trail was easy enough to follow, a clear path of crushed underbrush, and Fargo let the pinto push through on its powerful legs without forcing the horse. He was gaining ground, he knew, the Ovaro not only a stronger runner but moving along brush already stamped down. It wasn't long before he saw Jack Towers adding to his mistakes as he swerved his horse first one way, then the other. He was searching for thinner underbrush but his horse was beginning to tire. With each swerve he lost precious seconds, and Fargo drove straight forward as he picked up the sound of the other horse.

He came into a clear space and spotted Towers. He saw the man glance back and see the black-and-white horse flashing through the trees. Fargo saw him straighten his path and race forward, just avoid smashing into a half-fallen maple. For the first time in the pursuit, Fargo snapped the reins, and the pinto shot forward to quickly close the distance. Fargo drew the big Colt, took aim, and fired a single shot. It grazed the top of Jack Towers' hat and he saw the man rein up at once to come to a quick halt.

"That's being smart for a change," Fargo muttered as he rode up, sidled the horse next to Towers, and bound the man's wrists behind him. "Start back, a nice, slow trot," he said.

Towers, resignation gripping his face again, rode in front as he retraced steps.

"Trudy's idea, wasn't it?" Fargo asked, and Jack Towers nodded. Fargo fell silent, but his mouth was etched in disgust, and when they arrived back at the two big, leaning sycamores, Trudy was gone. But he'd expected that and he pulled Towers from the saddle, bound his ankles, and pushed him to the ground. "I'll be back," he snapped. "With Trudy." Towers looked at him with uncertain eyes. "It was a stupid move in the wrong place," Fargo said as he raced off.

Trudy's path west through the heavy brush was just as easy to pick up as Jack Towers' had been. She had more of a start, but it was the clear trail that mattered as he saw she'd made a long, slow circle to the north. He kept the Ovaro at a steady pace and saw that her horse had slowed, the brush growing more broken as it dragged legs through it instead of lifting them high. Trudy kept on north in terrain where he couldn't miss her tracks, where he had only to follow with dogged persistence. Wrong move in the wrong place, he murmured to himself. He was really very disappointed in her, he found himself thinking.

He rode on but the trail through the brush suddenly grew uneven, as if the horse were moving erratically through the trees. Fargo felt the frown dig into his brow as he leaned forward in the saddle. The trail swerved sharply to the right, halted, backed, and moved forward again, once more an uneven, erratic path. The frown dug in deeper as he followed the trail, and the oath was on his lips when he spotted the horse standing riderless, head down, nibbling at a patch of grass.

"Goddamn," he swore aloud as he halted, everything suddenly coming clear. She had slid from the saddle somewhere along the way while he'd followed the trail of the running, riderless horse. "Damn her hide," he bit out.

No mistakes at all on her part, only wily cleverness. She'd purposely chosen the spot to make him think she'd made a stupid move, a place where the trail would be so invitingly clear that he'd follow without hesitation. By now she was silently doubling back on foot.

He spun the Ovaro around and raced back through the heavy underbrush, certain what he'd find when he reached the spot where he'd left Jack Towers. He nodded with tight lips when he drew up and saw only the rawhide thongs left mockingly on the ground. She had planned every move, nothing done by mistake at all. She knew her brother would easily be caught, his move designed only to give her a chance to get away and leave another trail to follow.

She had drawn on everything he'd taught her, added a twist of her own, and turned it all around on him. He paused, held the Ovaro still, and his eyes grew narrow in thought. She had ridden with her brother, and by now they'd reached her horse. She counted on other things, though, Fargo mused—on his going after them and picking up their trail again. She also counted on the time they'd gain as he retraced steps and found their new trail and followed once more. But he wasn't about to play into her hands and do that, he told himself angrily. It was no longer simply a question of trail wisdom. He had to think as she thought, see her actions as she saw them, and that was part of trailing too.

She counted on his following the new trail, but she was proving far too smart to just hope to stay ahead. She'd move to shake loose of him once and for all, and that meant the ribbon of water in the distance. He turned the Ovaro west, racing through the brush. No more following, no more wasting time to pick up new prints. He settled into hard riding as the Ovaro made up precious minutes with each powerful, long stride. Trudy's damn wiliness stabbed at him again. The thought was grimly wry as it passed through his mind.

At least he wasn't disappointed in her any longer.

6

He was nearing the water when he crossed the hoofprints of the two horses, and he reined up when he reached the stream. It was deeper and wider than most, and he peered at the tracks that led into the water just as he'd expected they would. Once again, she was putting what she'd learned into effect.

But he wouldn't underestimate her now, and he followed into the stream as he scanned the banks upstream. The water marks were there, clear and fresh along the shore where the movement of the horses had sent ripples and spray to cause marks higher than they'd normally be. He rode upstream a few minutes, his eyes on the banks where the marks continued to show, and he suddenly reined to a halt. He had taught her how to tell whether a rider went upstream or down by the water marks. She damn well knew he'd see them.

He swore silently as he pulled the Ovaro around and rode downstream, halted to see the fresh water marks on the banks there also. She had sent her brother one way and herself the other.

Fargo stayed in place as thoughts tumbled through his head. She'd apparently left him with the choice of which way to follow. Only it wasn't really a choice. She wouldn't leave him with the chance of going after Jack just as she wouldn't leave Jack alone to be caught. Trudy intended to join up with her brother so she could use all she'd learned for the both of them. That meant she'd have to leave the stream someplace and double back on land, where she could ride faster than through the water. Fargo stared at the banks of the stream. He was still left with the task of deciding which way she had taken, upstream or down.

Once again it was no longer a matter of trails, prints, and marks. It was a question of understanding the ways of one's prey, just as one had to understand the cougar's ways to hunt the cougar. He was getting to understand Trudy—in ways he could do without, he grunted painfully. She saw herself as the savior, the only one who could outwit him for Jack, and she was probably right so far as that went. She'd let her brother take the easiest way, downstream with the current, Fargo decided, and turned the Ovaro around. He sent the horse upstream, staying in the middle of the stream as his eyes scanned the banks and the high water marks on both sides.

He'd gone on perhaps ten minutes when he slowed, his glance focusing on a long, flat rock that sloped downward to the stream, the perfect place for leaving the stream without a trail of telltale hoofprints in the soft bank. He took the Ovaro over to the edge of the rock and swung down from the horse and onto the stone. He crouched there as his eyes swept over the top of the flat rock, up from the part nearest the stream to the top and back down again. He saw nothing, but he remembered how she'd asked about leaving a stream without showing prints. He had told her about using flat rocks and how a horse's hooves could leave little bits of residue on the rock. He remembered how carefully she had taken it all in, and now he pressed his open palms against the top of the stone. He slowly moved them across the flat surface, and a grim smile came to his lips as his palms found the still-damp places. She had carefully cleaned away all the tiny bits of mud and weed, but she couldn't wipe away the dampness on the stone where wet hooves had stepped. This was where she'd left the stream to double back.

He walked back to the Ovaro, swung onto the horse, and left the stream. She would have thrown off most anyone else, he knew, and felt a strange combination of anger and pride. He nosed into the trees beyond the bank and picked up her hoofprints. She had doubled back along this side, riding hard, obviously confident she'd shaken him.

"Guess again, honey," Fargo muttered as he sent the Ovaro forward.

He followed her trail as the day came to an end and darkness forced him to break off the chase. They'd have to rest also, he knew as he dismounted and took down his bedroll. He slept well, satisfied that he'd catch up to Trudy before another twenty-four hours passed.

He was riding with the dawn, following Trudy's tracks again, and found where she joined her brother downstream perhaps two miles from where they'd gone into the water. The double tracks turned northwest then, and he continued at a steady pace. When the trail turned sharply to the west, he peered ahead and a smile touched his lips. Trudy was taking no chances, the tracks leading into a thick pine woods. He followed into the cool darkness and inhaled the bracing fragrance of the pines as he swung down from the Ovaro.

The trail of hoofprints had disappeared in the springy bed of pine needles that carpeted the woodland floor, just as Trudy expected. One more lesson she had absorbed too well, he grimaced. With the Ovaro following, he began to walk slowly through the pine woods, his eyes peering down at the tree trunks.

The soft and springy bed of pine needles allowed no hoofprints to remain, but as a horse passed near a tree, the needles against the base of the trunk were pushed upward where they lay, no longer flat, but pressed up against the trunk. Carefully, he scanned each tree for the little pine needles pushed up and against the base. It was agonizingly slow, but when the trail led in a fairly straight line, the task of following speeded up. Yet, he had to be careful, his eyes scanning the base of each tree trunk to be sure his quarry didn't turn. It was a piece of trail lore maybe only three men knew, two of them the Cherokee who had taught it to him.

The morning passed into noon and beyond when the pine woods came to an end and the prints of the two horses became clear in the open ground. He climbed back onto the pinto and sent the horse forward into a fast trot. Trudy and her brother had halted to rest, he noted as he rode after the prints, and stopped again at a small lake. They were riding slowly, Trudy clearly certain she had shaken loose of him once and for all. Fargo slowed the pinto as the hoofprints grew fresh and sharp, and he came into sight of a gentle hill thinly grown with low-branched scarlet haw.

He reached the base of the hill and started up when he caught sight of the two riders moving toward the top of the slope. He reined up, peered at the pair from beneath the branches of the first row of haws. They didn't glance back as they rode, and Fargo's lips tightened. They had no guns and he didn't want to use his. Most of all, he didn't want another chase to develop.

He turned the Ovaro and set off across the bottom of the hill to the far edge, found the base, and circled it at a gallop to the other side, where he again dropped from the horse. He took the Sharps from its saddle case and hurried along the base of the other side of the hill with the rifle. Running in a crouch, he glimpsed Trudy and her brother starting down the slope. He spied a long line of brush and dived behind it. He crawled forward behind the brush until he reached the center of the base of the hill, where he watched Trudy lead the way down toward him.

He stayed hunkered down behind the brush, letting the two move down closer. A few paces ahead of her brother, Trudy was almost directly in front of him now, and Fargo brought the rifle around, waited another moment, and let her ride another six feet closer. He rose from the bushes, the big Sharps raised to fire.

"Surprise," he said quietly, and enjoyed the sheer shock and astonishment that flooded into Trudy's pert face.

She stared at him with her lips parted, a parade of emotions rushing through her face: awe, incomprehension, shock, disbelief, all of them slowly sliding into a kind of benumbed glower.

"Get off," Fargo said, and Trudy slid from the horse and Jack Towers did the same.

Fargo's eyes speared Trudy as she lifted her head, the pugnacious determination inside her quick to surface again. "You learned well. You're good, damn good," he said to her. "But I'm better."

"Yes," she said finally, and there was a long sigh in the single word. "Damn you."

His laugh held a wry satisfaction in it as she glowered at him. He moved quickly, tied her hands behind her, and did the same with Jack Towers before letting them mount up again. He led the way south, and Trudy rode in silence, the bitter disappointment stark in her eyes.

Fargo set a fast pace, and the day was drawing to a close when they reached Thief River Junction. He led the way down the street toward the sheriff's office, halted, and untied Trudy's wrists a few yards from the doorway. Her brown eyes blinked and she broke her silence.

"You decide what you're going to tell them about me?" she asked.

"Yes." He nodded. "The truth."

She took in his answer and her lips tightened as she followed him to the sheriff's office. Sheriff Covey came hobbling outside as Fargo halted, his eyes going to Jack Towers first.

"Well done, Fargo," the sheriff said, drawing his six-gun and motioning the younger man into his office.

Fargo followed with Trudy to see the sheriff march Jack into a cell and slam the door shut. Sheriff Covey turned to him, a tiredness in his face, and his eyes went to Trudy.

"Trudy Towers," Fargo said, and the sheriff's eyes widened. "She was looking for her brother when she came across me on the trail," Fargo said.

"Where's Halloway?" the sheriff asked.

Fargo flicked a glance at Trudy. She stared straight ahead, her face tight. "Dead," he answered the sheriff, and the man's eyes questioned again. "We were on our way back. One shot, came from inside a cluster of trees. I never saw who fired it," Fargo said.

Sheriff Covey's lips pursed. "Strange." He frowned. "But he was a man with a lot of enemies. Maybe somebody saw an opportunity and took it."

"Maybe," Fargo said.

"You did real well, Fargo," the sheriff said. "I'll tell Judge Little. He's asked every day if Towers was back. He'll start the trial first thing tomorrow, you can be sure."

"I might look in," Fargo said, and turned.

He touched Trudy's arm and she followed him outside into the new night. She halted, faced him with her eyes grave.

"Thanks," she murmured.

"I said I'd tell the truth. That's what I did, no more, no less," Fargo answered.

"I love you for being what you are, and I hate you for bringing Jack in," Trudy said, her face unsmiling.

"You can't take half of a person," he told her. She made no reply and the hurt and anger stayed in her eyes. "What now?" he asked.

"Get a room. Be at the trial tomorrow. Think of some way to help Jack," she said, biting off each thought as she uttered it.

"Something with more sense than sass, I hope," Fargo said.

"Something with both," Trudy returned. "I'd like my Walker back now."

He peered hard at her and the defiance in her face. But he had no reason to keep the gun any longer, and he pulled it from his belt and handed it to her. "Don't do anything stupid," he warned, not ungently.

"Like expecting you to believe in me and my brother?" she snapped bitterly.

"Something like that," he said, turned from her, and walked away as the Ovaro followed after him. He felt the hurt and anger of her reaching out until he heard her boot heels stomp away. He stabled the Ovaro and paid the attendant to give the horse a good rubdown and then got a room at the boardinghouse-hotel. He undressed quickly and enjoyed the luxury of a bed.

He was tired, yet an unaccountable restlessness kept sleep away. Trudy's troubled eyes remained with him. But he knew that wasn't enough. There was more, something of inner senses instead of rational reason. Somehow, for some reason, the feeling of a job well done eluded him. Instead, he had the gnawing sense of something not right. Nothing he could pinpoint yet, just a sixth sense. And he had learned long ago not to dismiss inner feelings.

He let his mind go back over everything that had happened upon his arrival at Thief River Junction. He went over his first meeting with Sheriff Covey, the man's account of the murders, the appearance of Frank Halloway, the brief meeting with Judge Little. His thoughts strayed to the search and to Halloway's revelation that Judge Little had hired him, to his attempted killing of Jack Towers, and finally to the prisoner's account of his innocence.

Fargo found himself frowning into the darkness. There was nothing he could isolate, and yet something wasn't right. He couldn't put it together, but the nagging feeling refused to go away. It was as if he were being warned to think again, examine the situation more carefully. He felt as though he were looking at one of those drawings where faces and objects were hidden in the picture for you to find. You knew they were there and yet you couldn't see them without turning the drawing upside down and sideways, without freeing the mind of surface appearances.

He turned on his side and finally drew sleep around himself, shutting out the musings that provided nothing. He slept until the morning sun filtered through the lone window of the room. He washed, dressed, breakfasted downstairs on bacon, muffins, and coffee, then strolled down the street to the tattered building that carried the sign: COURTROOM.

Sheriff Covey stood outside and nodded to him as he approached. "Seats are damn near filled up," he told Fargo. "Seth Owens was an important man around here."

Fargo walked into the large room almost filled with onlookers seated on long, wood benches. A desk faced them from the front of the room, a big black gavel lying atop it. He saw the compact figure in a yellow blouse and black skirt standing against the wall, and her eyes went to him as he halted beside her.

"You always follow through with your work?" Trudy asked tartly.

"Always," he returned.

"Conscientiousness or conscience?" she snapped.

"Maybe some of both," he said, and she walked away to take the last seat at the end of a bench. He scanned the room again and saw the thin, wiry, small-torsoed figure with the black hair framing the straight-nosed, attractive face. He sat in the empty place beside her, and Alva Brown turned a soft smile at him.

"What are you doing here?" Fargo frowned.

"Irma Owens and I were friends," Alva said. "A terrible thing, all this." She dropped her voice to a whisper. "When are you coming by? I've been waiting," she said.

"Soon, real soon," he promised.

Judge Little's entrance into the courtroom ended any further talk. The man was clothed in a black robe that heightened the silver-haired handsomeness of his even-featured face. Judge Little banged the gavel three times as he faced the audience. "This court in the fourth district of the Territory of Minnesota is now in session," he intoned. "The people charge Jack Towers with the murder of Seth and Irma Owens."

Fargo watched Judge Little's eyes slowly roam the room.

"In the interests of time and quick justice, I will hear and try this case. The defendent will be given the chance to speak for himself."

The judge sat down, and Sheriff Covey appeared with Trudy's brother in manacles. He sat the young man on the wooden bench directly in front of the judge.

Judge Little began by calling the testimony of the two men who were there when Jack Towers was found holding Seth Owens' gun over the murdered man. He then added his own eyewitness testimony to the proceedings. When he finished, Sheriff Covey was called to testify that Jack Towers had fled to avoid standing trial and had eluded capture until brought in by a specially hired tracker.

Fargo listened intently, aware that the judge had set out all the factors to establish Jack Towers as guilty. That much was his role as judge and jury—establishing the facts and letting them fall into place as they would—and the territory laws didn't demand a jury to hang a man. Territory judges were empowered to try, hear, and judge all on their own. Even traveling judges had that power. He sat back as Judge Little turned to Jack Towers.

"You've heard the evidence against you," the judge said. "How do you plead?"

"Not guilty," Jack Towers said.

"Let's hear your side of it," the judge ordered with a trace of disdain in his tone. He seemed almost bored as he listened to the story Jack Towers told, exactly the same account the man had given him, Fargo noted. Once again, the picture was the same, but everything in it was drawn differently.

When Jack Towers finished his account of everything that had taken place, Judge Little fastened a cold stare on him. "All you give is your own word. We've witnesses that saw you bending over Seth Owens and running away from Irma Owens' body in front of her house," he said.

"Sam Delafeld can prove I was innocent," Jack Towers said.

"You keep saying that. Maybe he was in it with you. He's run away, just the way you did. Or maybe you're just saying he can clear you," the judge said. "It's just your word again, and that's not enough. You've no proof of anything you've said."

"You've no proof that I was seen running away from Irma's body. All you keep saying is that somebody saw me," Jack Towers countered.

Judge Little's silver hair glinted in a shaft of sunlight through the window as he turned his head, his handsome face showing a kind of disdainful weariness. "Will Alva Brown come up and be heard?" he said.

Fargo's brows lifted as Alva rose and brushed past him, her face set tight. She walked to the witness chair beside the desk and perched at the edge of it.

"Did you see Jack Towers running from Irma Owens' body?" the judge asked.

"Yes," she said, her voice small.

"How did you come to see this?" she was questioned.

"I was in my buckboard, driving by, when I saw him running away," Alva said, her eyes cast down at her hands folded in her lap.

"Are you sure it was Jack Towers you saw running away?" Judge Little asked.

"Yes," Alva said, her voice almost inaudible.

"You know you can be put in jail for lying in a courtroom, Alva," Judge Little cautioned.

"I'm not lying. I saw him running away," Alva said.

"That's all, thank you," Judge Little said, and Fargo watched Alva quickly leave the chair and return to sit beside him, her face still drawn tight.

"I hated to do that," she whispered to him.

"He called on you," Fargo said. "You had to tell it as it is." Alva nodded and Fargo lapsed into silence as he felt the strange, nagging uneasiness inside him again. There'd been nothing wrong in Alva's testimony that he could see, and yet there was something wrong about all of it. The certainty grew more and more firm inside him. Yet he still had absolutely nothing to take hold of, only an undefined something that refused to reveal itself. The hidden objects in the drawing again, they were there, somewhere, in all that he'd seen and heard. Judge Little's voice brought his attention back to the courtroom.

"Anyone else here want to speak for the defendant?" the judge asked. "If so, stand up and be heard now."

The room was silent until Trudy's voice cracked the uncomfortable stillness, and Fargo saw her get to her feet, all the pugnaciousness inside her shining from her snub-nosed face. "I'll speak for the defendant," she said crisply.

Judge Harvey Little's eyes fastened her with a long, appraising stare. "Name," he said.

"Trudy Towers. Jack is my brother," she said.

Judge Little's stare stayed on her. "You have any evidence to back up his story?" he asked.

"I will have," Trudy said, and the judge let one brow lift. "I'm going to find Sam Delafeld and bring him in."

"That's not courtroom evidence, young woman. That's just more talk," the judge snapped coldly.

"I'll find him. I just need the time. Two weeks," Trudy said.

"Out of the question," Judge Little said brusquely.

"Why? You're dealing with my brother's life here. I ought to be given a chance to prove his innocence," Turdy argued.

"The defendant, by his own words, hasn't been able to find Sam Delafeld in a month and a half," the judge said.

"I'm different. I'll find him," Trudy insisted.

"I think you're just stalling, trying to buy time until you can try some other way to free the defendant," Judge Little said sternly. "Well, that won't work, not in this courtroom."

"I can find him. The man who brought my brother in trained me. You can ask him yourself. He's right here in this courtroom," Trudy said.

Fargo kept the wry smile inside himself. She fought, battled, drew in help in whatever way she could. He found Judge Little's eyes on him and he got to his feet.

"Is that true?" the judge asked.

"Yes," Fargo said. "I taught her a good deal."

"You think she can find this man?" the judge asked.

Fargo half-shrugged. "If he can be found, I'd say she could do it," he answered.

He saw Judge Little's mouth tighten, a tiny moveınent at the corners of his lips as he returned his eyes to Trudy. "No matter, justice has been delayed entirely too long already in this case," he said.

"One week," Trudy cut in. "I deserve one week to save my brother's life."

"Twenty-four hours," the judge snapped, and pounded his gavel. "Court adjourned for now."

Fargo knew a frown had slid across his brow at the decision, and he watched the man stride from the courtroom. His eyes went to Trudy, and he saw the anger in her face as she stared into space. He couldn't blame her. She deserved a chance to try to save her brother, and the judge's decision hung in his thoughts.

Her request had been rejected out of hand, almost roughshod. The twenty-four hours Judge Little had given her perhaps satisfied some legal technicality on defendant's rights, and in the records it would go down as a last gesture on the court's part. But it was a meaningless gesture, Fargo knew. Alva's hand on his arm broke off his thoughts and he turned to her.

"Soon?" she half-whispered. "I've been wanting as much as waiting. Seeing you again was like opening up floodgates of memories."

"Soon," he promised, and she pressed his arm before hurrying away.

His glance went across the courtroom to find Trudy and saw she had gone. He walked outside, scanned the knots of people clustered outside. She wasn't among them, and he peered down the street and espied her compact figure striding away, short brown hair tossing as she walked. He strolled after her, not hurrying, and the thoughts he had had inside the courtroom returned to gnaw at him.

Little things spiraled into his mind, the first of them Jack Towers' insistence that he had been trapped, framed as a killer. Judge Little had been one of those who came upon him bending over Seth Owens, and it had been Judge Little who'd hired Frank Halloway. Moreover, Halloway had said the judge had told him he could bring in Jack Towers dead or alive. Fargo's lips pursed as he walked. Had Halloway been told more than that? Had he been told to bring the prisoner in dead? Was that why he was so determined to kill Towers? Perhaps it wasn't all one big coincidence, Fargo pondered. One thing was certain in his mind: the judge seemed in a big hurry to get Jack Towers into a hangman's noose.

He turned off thoughts as he saw Trudy go into the stable, and he was waiting outside when she emerged with her horse. A moment of surprise entered the dark anger of her eyes.

"What do you want here?" she asked.

"Wondering what you think you're going to do?" he asked.

"Find Sam Delafeld in twenty-four hours," Trudy snapped.

"How?" Fargo asked calmly.

"I'm not telling you anything. You're on their side," Trudy accused, but there was more striking out than anything else in her voice.

"I'm not on anybody's side—not yet, anyway," he said. "Where are you going?"

She glowered at him, her lower lip thrust out, but she answered. "Jack said Sam Delafeld lived in a hut up past Woodchuck Ridge. I'm going there. Maybe I'll find something, an address, a name, something that might help find him."

"Jack looked there, didn't he?" Fargo said.

"In a rush. He was being chased then. He had to look fast and run. Maybe he missed something. It's all I have. I've got to try," Trudy said.

"Guess you do," Fargo said.

"You could help me."

"You've a short memory. I already did that," he said.

Trudy flung an angry glare at him as she spun away, climbed onto her horse, and went off at a fast canter.

He strolled into the stable, paid the stableboy, and saddled the Ovaro. He rode out from the stable and left town unhurriedly. It wasn't necessary to pick up Trudy's tracks yet. She had to head north, into the low hill country, and she'd not reach Woodchuck Ridge till dark. He let his mind toy with other thoughts that pushed their way forward. The hidden faces in the picture were taking shape, little by little. Not enough for him to be sure of anything yet, but enough for him to wonder and search deeper.

Judge Little's haste hadn't been the only surprise. Alva's presence there had been another. She'd been called there to give testimony to what she had seen. Nothing wrong in that. That was simple and understandable enough. It was things never asked and never said that pushed at him, suddenly taking shape, surfacing at their own time. He broke off thoughts, swung the Ovaro in a wide circle that eventually led him back toward Woodchuck Ridge in the low hill country as the day began to wear to an end.

He picked up Trudy's tracks in the last light, and he entered a woods of mountain maple. He kept to the right of the tracks and finally spotted her in the distance. She was riding hard, and he followed by visual contact until the night came to cloak her in its blackness.

He rode over the low rise that was Woodchuck Ridge and halted as the moon rose to spread its paleness over the clear land below. A small yellow light broke the dimness in the distance, and Fargo rode forward as the hut took shape, the flickering light from a window, and he saw Trudy's horse outside.

Trudy had found a lamp, set it on, and was scouring the place, the lamplight dimming and brightening as she moved the lamp from place to place inside the hut. Fargo halted under a maple off to one side and took his eyes from the hut to focus his attention on the ridge. He wondered as he waited, half-hoped he'd be right for Trudy's sake and half-hoped he'd be wrong for the sake of decency and justice. He always felt a particular sour taste inside his mouth when the corrupt wore the robes of justice and law and order. He grimaced and turned off thoughts. It was still too soon to jump to conclusions.

The minutes dragged by, and Trudy still searched. Fargo was beginning to think that perhaps he had thought wrong when the three horsemen appeared atop the low ridge. He watched as they halted and gazed down at the hut just as the lamplight went out and Trudy emerged from the hut. She swung onto her horse and trotted away, a touch of aimlessness in the way she rode.

Fargo saw the three horsemen immediately separate as one rode fast along the top of the ridge, a second went south and started down, while a third moved downward directly toward Trudy. They were going to box her in, Fargo saw, and he waited and watched with his eyes narrowed. He stayed in place, his lips a thin line. He had to be certain, and that meant letting them get to Trudy.

As he watched, he saw Trudy half-turn when she spotted the rider coming down from the rise directly toward her. She slowed, almost halted, and then suddenly, instincts seizing hold of her, sent the horse into a gallop. But it was too late as the one that had raced along the ridgeline now came at her to block her path, and the third one drew up behind her. She whirled her horse, saw they had her boxed in, and reined to a halt. Fargo watched as one of the trio took her gun while another seized the cheek strap of her horse.

Trudy in the middle, they began to ride her away, and Fargo moved the Ovaro forward, following the men through a patch of haw to where a lake appeared as a silvered oval under the moon. They halted, pulled Trudy out of the saddle, and Fargo moved forward quickly as he unholstered the big Colt. He could hear their voices now as he reined up under a low branch, all their attention concentrated on Trudy.

"Don't hit her. It's supposed to look like an accident," one said to the others.

"You'll never get away with this," Trudy snapped with more hope than confidence.

"The hell we won't. It'll look just like your horse threw you and you drowned in the lake," one answered.

Fargo watched as they began to drag Trudy toward the water and she tried to kick and bite.

"Bastards. Rotten bastards," Trudy swore at them as they pulled her roughly, helplessly, to the edge of the water.

One of the men put an arm around her neck and started to push her down into the water.

"Just hold her under," another said.

Fargo moved the Ovaro into the open. "That's enough," he said, and saw the three men freeze, turn, one with his arm still around Trudy's neck. "Let her go," Fargo ordered.

"Son of a bitch," the man cursed. "Who the hell are you?"

"The tooth fairy. Let her go," Fargo repeated.

"Sure, I will," the man roared as he flung Trudy to the side and yanked at his gun. Fargo's shot smashed full into his chest before the man's gun left its holster, and he flew backward in a half-somersault to hit the water with a huge splash. Fargo's gun barked again as the man to Trudy's right drew his gun, his shot catching the man in the abdomen. The figure doubled over almost in two as he pitched forward onto his face.

"Don't shoot," the third one called out as he half-crouched.

Fargo's Colt pointed directly at him as Trudy pulled herself to her feet. Fargo saw her start for the man, her face wreathed in fury.

"No, stay away from him," Fargo called to her, but Trudy ignored him as she attacked the man, one arm swinging out in an arc.

"Drown me, you bastard," Trudy shouted as she tried to rake the man's face with her nails.

Fargo swore at her as he saw the man step under the blow, spin, and seize her from behind, his arm circling her neck. Fargo caught the glint of gunmetal as the man brought his gun up under her arm, and he dived out of the saddle as the shot barely missed him. He hit the ground, rolled twice into a low line of brush, and looked up to see the man had dragged Trudy into the lake with him. Fargo half-rose, tried to find a place to shoot, but the man kept Trudy securely in front of him.

"Throw the gun out or I finish her," the man shouted, panic in his voice.

"She's the only thing keeping you alive, cousin," Fargo answered. "Shoot her, and you're dead for sure. Guaranteed."

The man's silence was its own answer. "Back off," he said, finally. "Back off, dammit."

Fargo paused, his lips drawn tight. The man was

aware Trudy was his protection and his problem. He wouldn't shoot her, not on purpose. But he was stretched tight. Anything could make him pull the trigger by accident. Fargo backed farther from the shore, the Colt held ready to fire, and he saw the man begin to drag Trudy through the shallow water toward where his horse waited on the bank.

"Let her go and stay alive," Fargo called.

"Just stay back, mister, stay way back," the man answered, and Fargo heard the fear in his voice.

Fargo stayed in place as the man reached his horse, disappeared around the other side with Trudy. A moment later, Trudy appeared as she climbed onto the horse, the gun in her back, and Fargo dropped to one knee as the man climbed into the saddle behind her. The man fired two wild shots back as he sent the horse into a gallop and raced down the edge of the lake.

Fargo holstered the Colt, yanked the big Sharps from its saddle holster as he vaulted onto the Ovaro and sent the pinto after the fleeing horseman. The man stayed in the clear as he tried to make time, and Fargo bent low over the Ovaro's neck as the horseman fired another shot back at him. Four, Fargo counted silently, including the first one he'd fired from in the water. Four wasted shots, the result of panic.

He stayed low as the pinto closed in fast with his powerful, thrusting strides. The man fired again and Fargo swerved the Ovaro to the right. Five, he grunted as he raced closer, paralleling the fleeing horse. He let the pinto close to where he was almost abreast of the man, saw the other horse skid almost to a halt as the reins were pulled back hard. The man raised his gun to take aim, and Fargo slid around to the side of the Ovaro's neck, clung there with his left arm as the shot whistled only inches over the saddle.

"Six," Fargo bit out as he pulled himself back into the saddle and sent the Ovaro swerving at the other horse. He raised the rifle, stock first, and smashed it into the man's head as he came alongside. The figure disappeared over the side of the horse and almost dragged Trudy along too, but Fargo saw her clutch a handful of the horse's mane and hang on. He yanked the Ovaro to a halt and leapt from the saddle as the man picked himself up, one side of his head streaming blood. He reached a hand inside his shirt and drew it out clutching a small pistol, foreign-made, Fargo could see. He brought the gun up to fire at point-blank range, and almost reluctantly Fargo pressed the trigger of the big Sharps. The man seemed to tear in half as the heavy burst of rifle fire slammed into him, and arcing backward, he hurtled back to land half in the water, which began to instantly run red. His pistol had fallen to the ground, and Fargo stepped to it, saw an English double-action Beaumont-Adams.

He looked up as Trudy returned on the horse, slid to the ground, and came against him, her head on his chest.

"Don't you ever listen?" he growled.

"I was mad," she murmured.

"You're always mad," Fargo grunted.

Her face lifted, eyes searching his. "You were there. You followed me. You suspected something and followed me," she said.

"Had to find out for myself," he said.

"Did you?" she questioned.

"Enough. Somebody wanted to make sure you weren't lucky enough or good enough to find Sam Delafeld," Fargo said.

"Judge Little?" Trudy asked.

"Can't say that. But somebody," Fargo said.

"I didn't find anything in the hut," Trudy told him. "What happens now?"

"I'll have to think some on that. First, let's find a place to bed down till morning," he said.

"My twenty-four hours will be up, come midday," she said.

"I know that," he said. "And there's no way we can find Sam Delafeld by then. Let's get away from here."

Trudy nodded, and they returned to the other end of the lake to retrieve her horse. They rode south until Fargo found a circle of Canada balsams and made camp. He set out his bedroll, turned around to see Trudy with her blouse off, starting to shed her skirt, breasts pale-white cones of loveliness in the moonlight. She slid into the bedroll with him as he threw off clothes. Her mouth found his, pressed hungrily, pulled away to scan his face.

"Damn you, Fargo," she murmured. "You keep making me love you and hate you and love you again."

"Which one is this?"

"Guess," she said as her lips found his, her tongue darting out, thrusting, sucking, demanding. Her hand dropped down to find his already swelling maleness, and she gasped in pleasure. She ran her hands up and down his body as she pressed herself against him, her wanting almost desperate, made up of a myriad of conflicting emotions and, above all, the hunger of the flesh.

His hand caressed her breasts, their very touch exciting, and he brought his leg up between her thighs. He pressed farther upward until he rested against the dark portal. He felt the warm moisture of her, already flowing, sending a surge of excitement through him at its touch.

"Oh, oh, yes," Trudy whispered as he caressed her, then brought himself atop her.

Her fingers dug hard into his shoulders as he slid into her slowly, deeply, pushing still more deeply, and she groaned. Her compact, rounded body exploded with desire, all its pugnacious energy channeled into the sensuousness of the moment. He cupped hands around her rear, pressed hard, and she pumped against him as she cried out.

"Yes, yes, yes," Trudy gasped. "More, more, Fargo, please more."

There was no waiting for his reply as her round body pumped and pressed, pushed and thrust, and her breasts slapped into his chest. She was all explosion, the flesh a servant of the senses, and when her quivering thrustings suddenly turned into spasms, her voice rose, wound itself into a spiral as she clung to the apex of ecstasy. When the cry ended, it snapped off in midair and she fell back breathing heavily, but her thighs still clasped around his waist.

"So, so wonderful," Trudy said breathlessly. "More wonderful each time."

"The wanting in between helps," Fargo said as he drew away and lay down beside her.

She cradled herself against him and lay still, but he knew she did not sleep. He lay awake too, his mind slowly bringing itself back to the things that needed doing and the plans that had to be formed, and formed correctly. She showed more patience than he had expected of her, but finally he felt her move, her head lift to rest against his chest as her eyes searched his face.

"What happens tomorrow?" she asked.

"You stay here, stay out of sight. Somebody thinks

you're dead. I want them to keep thinking that," Fargo said. "I'll be in the courtroom."

"To do what?" Trudy asked.

"Light a bonfire, let it smoke out the rats," Fargo answered. "That might take a day or two."

"I can't just sit here on my hands, not knowing anything," Trudy protested.

"You can and you will. It'll be good practice. You could use the self-discipline," Fargo told her, and received a glower. "I'll stop back if I possibly can."

"You'd better," she muttered.

"Now let's get some sleep," he said, taking her into his arms.

She came against him and was asleep in moments, and he slept with her until the new sun woke him. When he was dressed and in the saddle, he fastened a stern gaze on her half-pout.

"You keep out of sight here. That's an order, one you'd damn well better keep. It's important they think I'm on my own and you're out of the picture."

"All right," Trudy agreed through the half-pout.

He rode from the circle of balsams, looked back to see how they quickly closed her away inside. It was probably the safest spot for her, he told himself as he put the pinto into a canter.

When he finally reined up in front of the courthouse, he went inside. He found it filled again, but Alva was not among the crowd. The sheriff brought Jack Towers in, and Judge Little appeared, announced the court as being in session, and peered sharply around the room.

"Miss Trudy Towers," he called out, and waited. There was a long moment of silence. Fargo saw Jack Towers' frown in apprehension as he sought to find Trudy in the court. The judge called her name again and swept the room with a stern glance.

"She's not here. I must assume she didn't find Sam Delafeld. The twenty-four-hour extension granted by the court is over," Judge Little intoned.

"I found Sam Delafeld," Fargo said, rising to his feet. He saw Judge Little's handsome face flush with surprise. A frown followed as he stared back.

"Will you repeat that, Mr. Fargo?" the judge said.

"I said I found Sam Delafeld," Fargo said.

"How did you come to do this?" the judge asked, each word careful.

"Trudy asked me to see if I could, said she'd pay me for it," Fargo answered evenly.

"Where is Miss Towers now?" the judge asked.

Fargo shrugged. "Search me. Haven't seen her since yesterday. She went off on her own," he said.

Judge Little sat back in his chair, his eyes small, hard pinpoints of thought as he kept his gaze fixed on the big man in front of him. "Is Sam Delafeld here, ready to give testimony?" the judge questioned.

"No, he won't come in unless I can promise him he won't be held or accused of anything," Fargo said.

"Where is he?" the judge probed.

"He made me promise I wouldn't say," Fargo returned.

"This is most unusual." Judge Little frowned.

"He's sort of unusual," Fargo commented.

"What if you can't give him a promise such as that?" Judge Little queried.

"He'll be off and running again," Fargo said nonchalantly.

Judge Little's lips pursed in thought before commenting. "You're asking the court to promise things it may not be right to promise," he said finally. "What if his testimony really doesn't clear the prisoner? What if it turns out that he obviously was involved?"

Fargo shrugged noncommittally. "That's your decision," he said calmly. "I'm just telling you that if I don't go back with the promise he wants, you won't be seeing him in this courtroom."

"I see," the judge said, the frown still on his brow. "I'll have to take this new development under consideration before proceeding with the trial. Court is adjourned for now."

He rose, hurried from the courtroom with only one bang of the gavel, and the murmur of conversation immediately filled the air as the spectators began to file outside. Fargo saw Jack Towers frowning at him as he was led away by Sheriff Covey, concern and confusion in his eyes.

Fargo strolled from the courtroom and went to the hotel, where he took a room and undressed to his Levi's. He sat down on the bed and went over the morning in his mind. It had gone pretty much as he'd expected. He had lighted the bonfire with the courtroom packed, his words heard by the judge and everyone else. Someone would have to make a move. He had set himself up as the target. He now held the key to keeping Sam Delafeld out of the courtroom. If he couldn't deliver the promise, Jack Towers was as good as hung.

Fargo rose, wedged a chair against the door to the room, undressed fully, and stretched out on the bed. It seemed as good a time as any to catch up on some sleep.

7

Fargo rode the Ovaro slowly, almost at a walk, through the dark of the night. He had let the night grow late before he woke, left the hotel room, and headed from town. He'd ridden carefully, circled twice, doubled back once, making certain he wasn't being followed. He neared the circle of balsams now, still riding slowly, and he saw Trudy as he entered the trees, the Walker raised in her hand. She lowered the gun when she recognized the Ovaro, and he halted, swung down from the horse. Her arms encircled him at once.

He sat on the ground beside her as he told her what he had put forth in the courtroom, and she listened with her hand pressed hard into his arm.

"Now we wait," he said when he finished. "Somebody's got to make a move."

"What do I do?" Trudy asked.

"You stay holed up here, out of sight and out of trouble," he told her.

"This is driving me crazy," Trudy protested.

"You want to find out the truth? Then don't get in

the way," Fargo snapped harshly. "I'll try to stop back tomorrow night. Don't panic if I don't. I'll have to go with whatever might happen."

"When do I panic? After one night? Two nights? Three?" she jabbed back.

"You'll know. You'll feel it inside. For now, separate impatience from instincts," Fargo said as he rose to his feet, and pulling her with him. Her lips found his, soft pliancy that clung till he pulled back.

"Can't you stay?" she said, half-pouting.

"I want them to see me at the hotel, the Ovaro outside. I don't want anyone out looking for me," Fargo said.

"Be careful. God, be careful," Trudy murmured as she let him climb onto the pinto.

The circle of balsams with their dense branches quickly swallowed her up as he rode away. The trip back to town was quiet, and he tethered the Ovaro in front of the hotel and started for his room when he heard the elderly desk clerk call out.

"This was left for you, Mr. Fargo," the man said, and offered a small, light-blue square of notepaper folded over once and sealed with a thin line of wax. He went to his room before he opened it and read the neat, even hardwriting.

Fargo . . .
Can you come by tomorrow night? The waiting's beginning to hurt.

Alva

Fargo lay back across the bed and let the note fall onto the bedcover. A half-smile touched his lips. He'd visit Alva if nothing else happened. He had promised her. It was a time for keeping promises.

He stretched out across the bed, closed his eyes, and let his mind return to that first visit to Alva's house. His mind freed itself of unimportant things as he dredged impressions from his inner consciousness where, as always with him, they had lodged. He shuffled through the array of things absorbed but unnoted, taken in and simply stored away. He lay quietly for a long time as he pulled all the little things into place out of the storehouse of the inner mind. As always, he felt a stab of surprise at how well they pieced together their own pattern. Finally, he undressed and slept.

He stayed in bed late, let the morning wear on before he finally rose, washed, and breakfasted, then slowly strolled through town. He was aware that he drew a few glances from those who'd been in the courthouse, and he saw Sheriff Covey beckon to him as he passed the General Store.

"Jack Towers has been asking to talk to you, Fargo," the sheriff said.

"There's nothing to talk about yet," Fargo said.

"He keeps asking if anybody's seen his sister?" the sheriff mentioned.

Fargo shrugged. "Guess she's still out looking," he said.

"You sure set things on end in court yesterday, Fargo," the sheriff said.

Fargo shrugged again. "Unexpected things have a way of doing that." He smiled and strolled on.

In time, he returned to the hotel room and let the day turn to night before he left the room again. On the Ovaro, he rode slowly and again made certain he wasn't being followed, though he didn't expect that. The caution was more confirmation than anything else, and he finally neared Alva's neat house. He took in a line of tall, thin birches that stretched in front of the house and the row of rhododendron hedges extending to the pigsty fences at one side. He tethered the Ovaro to a fencepost at the side of the house.

Alva opened the door as he reached it, her arms around him at once, brown eyes very wide and very serious. "Fargo, oh, God, Fargo," she murmured into his chest.

"Couldn't resist an invite like that," he said.

Alva pushed the door closed after him as he stepped into the house. "I couldn't help it," she said, and looked away, almost ashamed.

He brought her face around to him. "That's what I was hoping," he said gently.

Alva's arms slid around his neck as she stepped into the adjoining room, where he saw the brass bed. Her thin, wiry body pressed against him as she guided him to it. Her wide eyes searched his face and and she lifted a hand to touch his cheek. "I want you, Fargo. God, I want you so bad it hurts," she said.

"I can't stay the night," he told her.

"I didn't expect so. You want to be in town in case they call for you," Alva said, and he nodded. "Then we have to make every minute count." She stepped back, pulled off the brown housedress she wore, and stood naked in front of him.

He smiled as memories pulled at him: her wiry, small-boned figure unchanged, the small breasts with their pale-pink nipples thrusting outward charged with a sharp sexuality, her flat abdomen and the dense nap of curly, tangled mat. She stood with her legs slightly apart, her thighs thin-fleshed loveliness.

He shed clothes, and Alva stepped forward to press herself against him. He felt the electric warmth of her spreading outward, joining with his flesh, radiating desire with shimmering waves. Again, memories flooded over him. It had always been that way with

Alva, her body gathering electric intensity, reaching out with an excitement that sent his loins churning.

She moved back onto the bed and he went with her. He felt her breasts push into his chest, each tiny nipple grown into soft firmness, each breast beautifully curved. He felt her lean legs come over his torso, rub up and down across his groin.

"Fargo. Ah, ah," Alva murmured, the sound a sibilant hiss. Her hands caressed his body as her legs slid back and forth across him. He felt her electricity crackling between her flesh and his, transforming her entire body into a sinuous lightning rod that quivered and vibrated. She half-lifted herself along his hard-muscled frame and thrust one small breast deep into his mouth. He heard her groans of pleasure as she pressed herself into his sucking caress. Alva groaned again, and he felt her entire body tremble.

He turned with her, still holding her breast in his mouth, and came over her. Her lean thighs drew up to embrace his hips at once, and he felt the fuzzy tangle against his belly. He reached down, touched the dark and warm places, and Alva's body trembled with desire.

"Yes, oh, yes. Fargo. The way it was. Oh, yes."

He remembered how it was, how she enjoyed and became transformed, and he pushed hard suddenly. Alva's scream exploded, and her furious quaking and quivering shook the bed. He thrust hard, again and again, and she cried out in pleasure as her thin, wiry body seemed to be ready to come apart with the tremendous quivering of every part of her. But Alva pulled against him, pushed the firm little breasts hard into him, and her tembling only increased as he surged and drew back and surged again inside her.

"Yes, oh, more, again, again," Alva cried out, her

voice rising, and he felt the tremendous trembling inside and outside her as she arched herself backwards, her thin neck curving until blue veins stood out. And when it seemed as though mere flesh could stand no more pleasure, she grew rigid, the trembling snapping off. A long, crying scream came from inside her and hung in the air, and Fargo heard the complete and utter release inside it, the senses satisfied in that one and only special satisfaction.

He sank down atop her as she grew limp, turned her face to push the black hair aside. Her hand brought his face down against the upwardly curved breasts and held him there. He listened to her slow, hissed gasps, each holding the echo of ecstasy, and when he finally drew from her, she gave a tiny murmur of protest.

"Only with you," Alva murmured. "Reality as wonderful as memory." She turned again, rolled over to lay beside him, and looked small suddenly, yet the wiry, electric strength of her still there in the lean tightness of her body.

"You did right well yourself," Fargo said, and Alva's smile was filled with sadness.

"Thank God for that," she said.

"You were afraid it wouldn't be what it was once," Fargo said. "Understandable."

"We change, Fargo, old lover. Life changes us, beats on us until we stop caring about anything except making it through another day," Alva said.

"Some trees break, some bend and snap back," Fargo said.

Fargo met Alva's eyes as they stayed on him, wide and grave and filled with their own racing thoughts, their normally wide-eyed expression more so than usual. He pushed himself up to a sitting position and started to draw on trousers.

"I'd best get back," he said. "But you can bet I'll be coming around again. We'll have plenty of chance to turn the clock back again."

Alva's eyes stayed on him as he finished dressing, and she swung from the bed only when he strapped his gun belt on. He cupped a hand under her small face.

"Run out of words?" He smiled.

"I guess so," she murmured, standing naked before him, looking suddenly waiflike.

"Some things don't change. Some do. It's as simple as that, Alva," he said, and she stepped back, drew on the brown housedress as he took three long strides to the door. His hand rested on the latch when Alva's voice pierced the silence, a sharp, strangled cry.

"No! Don't!"

Fargo, his hand still on the latch, turned to her.

"Don't go out there," Alva said as her voice cracked.

Fargo's face had become chiseled stone. "Why not?" he flung back. "Because the judge and his hired guns are out there waiting for me?" He watched as Alva's face mirrored shocked surprise. Her eyes stayed on him, round and wide, filled with dark pain.

"Yes," she murmured finally. "Yes, they're out there." A tiny frown furrowed her brow as she continued to stare at him. "And you knew. You knew all along."

Fargo nodded solemnly. "I had to find out if you were going to let me open that door," he said.

Alva stepped forward, flung herself against him, and buried her face in his chest. "I couldn't. I couldn't. Oh, God, never," she said.

"But you brought me here. You followed orders," Fargo said coldly.

"Only the note. Nothing else was following orders, Fargo. You've got to believe that," Alva entreated.

It was true, he was certain, her desperate desire far beyond faking. "That doesn't change the rest," he said.

"No, it doesn't," she agreed. "How did you know?"

"Little things that I began to fit into place," Fargo said. "That first day I came by, you kept saying how surprised you were to see me. But you never once asked me what I was doing up in this country, not once. It didn't bother me at the time, but it sat inside me, like something undigested. When I saw you at the trial, it came back to me. You never asked because you knew why I was up here. You knew I'd been called to track down Jack Towers, and that put you on the inside someplace."

Alva nodded, bitterness in her face. "Yes, too deep inside," she murmured.

"Judge Little's your Thursday-night caller, isn't he?" Fargo asked.

"Yes, but still not the way you make it sound. I didn't lie about that to you," she said.

"Suppose you tell me about it," Fargo said.

"Judge Little and Seth Owens were stealing the town treasury blind. When Seth Owens wanted more of a share, the judge decided to get rid of him. But he wanted a killer all ready to hang," she explained.

"So he arranged to make that Jack Towers," Fargo supplied.

Alva nodded. "Only Towers ran away. They were afraid he'd eventually find Sam Delafeld and prove himself innocent, but they couldn't track him down. That's when they sent for you."

"How do you fit in, Alva?" Fargo questioned.

"Judge Little and Seth Owens couldn't risk keeping

the money they stole each week at their homes. They needed someplace safe to bring it. What better place than a pig farm? Nobody comes snooping around a pig farm."

The judge delivered a little bundle every Thursday night," Fargo said, and Alva nodded again, her hands moving with a tiny helpless motion. "That testimony you gave about seeing Jack Towers run from Irma's body, a lie ordered by Judge Little?" Fargo asked.

"No. I was driving by and I did see him running," Alva said. "But I heard the shot from the trees that killed Irma. I just said nothing about that." She stepped back and her eyes were filled with inner twistings. "I was paid well for storing the money. It became easier and easier to look the other way. I was only a storehouse. I wasn't involved, I lied to myself. I knew better, of course, but when I saw how powerful Judge Little had become, I was too afraid to tell anyone. I was trapped." Alva turned away to stare at the wall, her hands clenched into fists at her side. "Only there comes a time when you have to face yourself, when you have to stop. My time was called Fargo," she said softly.

He stepped to her, put his arms around her from behind. "I'm glad for that," he told her gently. She turned, pressed his arms to her. "Where's the money? In one of the pigpens?" Fargo asked.

"I don't have it anymore," Alva said, and drew a frown of surprise. "He's hidden all of it in sacks beneath a pile of logs on a raft tied up at Thief River."

"Why?" Fargo questioned.

"He's taking no chances. If he can hang Jack Towers and tie it all up neatly, he'll go on using his office to steal from the town treasury. If he can't, he knows he'll have to run. Everything will come out in the open, and and they'll chase after him. They won't be looking for a raft of logs sailing downriver."

"Covered all the bases for himself, hasn't he?" Fargo grunted with bitter admiration.

"Including you," Alva said. "Why did you come here? You're trapped now. You knew, and yet you came and let yourself be trapped. I don't understand it."

"There are traps and traps. You can get out of some," Fargo told her.

"There's only one door out of here, Fargo. They'll shoot you the minute you run through it. There's no other way out," Alva said.

"Guess again," Fargo answered as he unbuckled his gun belt and began to shed his clothes.

Alva stared at him as he quickly undressed, her frown deepening as, in moments, he stood before her with his magnificently muscled body naked.

"Sometimes you undress to get in, sometimes to get out," he said.

"Have you gone mad?" Alva frowned.

"Like a fox. I remembered noticing that you haven't been using your fireplace," Fargo said.

"Won't be until the real cold sets in. Got a wood stove for cooking," Alva said.

"Which means that your chimney will be cold. Full of soot but cold," he said as he tied his gun belt around his clothes, rolled it all into a neat bundle.

"You're going to go up the chimney," Alva gasped, and took in the breadth of his shoulders. "If you fit," she murmured.

"I'll find a way to fit. Now get me some rope," he said.

When she'd fetched a length of cord, he tied the clothes and gun belt securely, fashioned a loop, and put it around his neck so that the neat bundle hung down to his waist, leaving both his hands free for climbing. Finished, he turned to Alva.

"I'm going to tie you," he told her. "When I don't come out by morning they'll have to come in looking. It'll look better for you if they find you tied. You just tell them I'd figured out part of it and made you tell me the rest."

Alva nodded, and when he finished tying her, he put her in a corner of the room, stepped to the fireplace, and bent over low to fit himself inside it. He gazed up at the black funnel, straightened, and his head reached into the bottom of the blackness. The acrid smell of soot and smoke-blackened stone immediately assailed his nostrils. The stones were set together irregularly with enough creviced places to afford hand- and toeholds. It wouldn't be a long climb, but it promised to be thoroughly nasty. Maybe impossible, he grimaced but refused to hold the thought. He ducked down, looked across the room at Alva, and saw the concern and hope for him in her eyes.

"Till next time, honey," he called softly, drew a deep breath, and began the climb up inside the chimney.

The opening was indeed narrow; and he almost didn't fit, his body rubbing along the sides. It made climbing more difficult, for he had to keep his arm raised, outstretched after each hold. He used the strength in his fingers and hands as he started until he had climbed far enough to find a toehold on the uneven rocks. But he hadn't climbed more than a few feet when the loosened soot began to fill the chimney, far thicker and more choking then he'd expected. It blanketed him, filling every inch of the chimney almost instantly with its acrid, sharp odor. He closed his eyes and breathed through his nose, but in a few moments the chimney was filled with choking, suffocating soot. It covered him as he laboriously continued to climb. With every inch, he stirred more of it loose from the blackened stones.

He felt it go up into his nostrils, clogging, blocking air passages, and he began to climb more quickly, realizing that time had become all important. He dug his fingers into the stones, clutching at every little hold he could. He pressed hard with his toes to push himself upward. There wouldn't be another try, he knew, the chimney impassable with the swirling soot. He felt the terrible tightening in his chest as lungs began to strain to the breaking point, and a wry thought became a spur to his struggles. He'd be black as the night when he reached the roof. The waiting killers would never see him.

He found another narrow strip of stone with his fingers and pulled. But his chest was circled by ever-tightening steel bands now, and he felt almost disoriented as the total blackness and the suffocating soot turned time and space into a stygian void. Only the touch of the stones reminded him where he was, and he felt a wave of dizziness sweep over him.

The soot was so fine it penetrated his ears, nostrils, the very pores of his skin. Another wave of dizziness surged over him when he felt something else, a touch of coolness filtering downward. He shook away the pain in his chest. He had to be near the top, and he drew on a last burst of willpower and muscle, dug fingers into a ledge of stone, and pulled. The draft of air grew suddenly stronger, blew down again, and he paused to breathe and gagged on the soot he drew in. But night air came with it to flood into his lungs, and the steel bands snapped from around his chest.

He paused, once again pulled himself upward, and he felt the air against his face. He opened his eyes, shook soot from the lids and saw that he was at the top of the chimney. Slowly, he lowered himself over the edge and onto the slanted roof, drawing in deep breaths and flexing the arching tendons of fingers, hands, arms, and shoulders. When his breath had returned to normal, he looked down at himself and saw he was completely coated with soot, blackened from head to toe, and he smelled like a charred log.

His gaze moved down to the ground outside the door of the house and he found the figures waiting, strung out along the hedge and backed up against the trees. Three, he counted, and it was too dark to pick out features. Silently, Fargo slid to the back edge of the roof, lowered himself over the side, and dropped to the ground. Silent as a black panther, he moved his blackened nakedness to where the Ovaro waited at the side of the house. He saw the horse's ears go up at the smell of the unfamiliar, burnt odor, and the Ovaro backed nervously. Fargo reached out, laid his hand alongside the horse's ribs, and let the animal respond to the touch and feel he knew. The horse quieted down immediately.

Fargo stepped forward, untied the reins from the fence post, and began to back the horse from alongside the house. He heard the whispered voice from the hedges.

"The horse," the voice called, and Fargo stayed beside the Ovaro's head as he let the horse have free rein to move out.

"He's just walking around," Fargo heard another voice answer. "There's nobody there with him."

Fargo waited a moment, gave the horse more rein, and slowly edged his way alongside him. He kept the horse at a slow walk until his blackened body melted into the birches with the Ovaro. Only then did he swing himself up into the saddle and walk the horse forward. He went into a slow trot when he was certain he was out of earshot, and he rode across country before swinging north to head toward Trudy.

He peered through the night and finally caught the silver sparkle of moonlight on water, veered to his left, and sent the Ovaro galloping. He reached the lake, flung the bundle of clothes aside, and dived from the back of the horse into the water feetfirst. Flinging himself forward, he dived under the surface.

He swam underwater for a half-dozen yards and surfaced to see the round, spreading sphere of soot clinging to the top of the water. He dived again, feeling the cool lake wash him clean, and he came up and strode onto the shore and walked to the Ovaro. He yanked a towel from his saddlebag, dried himself quickly as the night air chilled his wet skin. He dressed and climbed back onto the pinto no longer feeling like a chimney sweep. He sent the Ovaro north again until he finally reached the circle of balsams.

The moon had begun to slip to the edge of the night horizon when he rode to a halt. He saw Trudy sit up on her bedroll, the Walker in one hand as she wiped sleep from her eyes. She was up and in his arms in one, long leap, clinging hard against him.

"I can't do it anymore. I can't sit here alone waiting," she said. "I'm not ready for that kind of self-discipline."

"You probably won't ever be," Fargo remarked. "No matter now, the waiting's done with."

Trudy peered hard at him as she pulled back. "You found out something. Tell me," she said.

"I was right, bonfires attract insects," he said. "They came, waiting to strike. They're still waiting." He eased himself down on a corner of the bedroll and stretched muscles still sore and aching.

Trudy dropped to her knees beside him.

He began with his visit to Alva and the suspicions he had when he went there. He supplied a carefully edited version of the visit. Details were unimportant, he told himself. And dangerous, knowing Trudy. He went on to how Alva had been unable to let him open the door to leave and continued with the rest of it pretty much as Alva had told him. He finished with the climb up the chimney to escape.

"We go the sheriff now?" Trudy queried.

"No," Fargo answered.

"You think he's in it, too?" she pressed.

"No, I don't. Alva would've told me if he was. But Sheriff Covey's a careful man. He won't just take our word. He'll want to talk to Alva, check the treasury, satisfy himself."

"And Judge Little will be free and clear by then," Trudy supplied.

"If I don't stop him," Fargo said. "He's found out things have come apart by now. He's no doubt hightailing it already. But I know where he's heading. He has the money hidden on a raft at Thief River."

"How appropriate," Trudy snapped bitterly.

Fargo lay back across the bedroll, put hands behind his back, and closed his eyes as dawn began to streak the sky.

"You going to sleep now?" Trudy protested.

"I'm going to think," Fargo said. "If I can get some quiet." His eyes still closed, he let thoughts parade through his mind, slowly sorting the things he knew from the things he surmised, and let plans slowly form out of both. Maybe the judge planned to run on his own, but it was more likely he'd have the two gunslingers from outside Alva's house. There'd not likely be more. A raft didn't allow for much of a crowd. But the judge was as clever as he was crooked.

A raft in midriver would be a floating island, hard to get at but giving him the chance to slip off unseen in the night. Fargo grunted at the thought. He couldn't give Judge Little that choice. Eyes staying closed, he let thoughts drift on and plans slowly took shape. They soon crystallized in his mind. He let himself half-doze for a spell as he renewed energies, and when he finally snapped his eyes open, he saw Trudy standing beside the dark mare, impatience in her face.

He pushed himself to a sitting position and saw the morning sun had already taken charge of the new day. "Sit down," he said.

"Finished your thinking?" Trudy asked, and he nodded. "I'm going along, no matter what you've come up with," she tossed at him with her usual pugnaciousness.

"That's one more thing you've got to learn," Fargo sighed.

"What is?" Trudy glowered.

"How to hold your tongue," Fargo snapped. "Maybe I was going to include you anyway."

"I wanted to be sure," she snapped, paused, then searched his face. "Were you?" she asked, and somehow managed to seem instantly vulnerable.

"Yes," he barked. "You've come this far to clear your brother. You deserve to see it through."

She came toward him, dropped to her knees beside him and looked contrite. "Thanks." Trudy murmured.

"Besides, I need you to make it work," he said, and saw her lips tighten instantly.

"Damn you, Fargo," she hissed.

"It'll mean risking your neck again." He laughed. "If Judge Little gets away, Jack will always be under

8

Fargo rode the Ovaro just inside the trees that bordered Thief River. Judge Little had sailed his raft south downriver with the current, he was certain. The judge would have made good time, the current fairly swift. Fargo figured, and he increased the Ovaro's pace. He swung out of the trees to ride in the clear along the bank for a few minutes and then returned into the treeline. He hadn't seen Trudy, and he nodded in satisfaction at that. But she was there, on the opposite bank, staying inside the trees just as he was. He'd stayed in the open only long enough for her to see that he'd picked up the pace, and he rode through the trees again as the Thief River made a slow curve westward.

The river came out of its curve, its tree-lined banks widening, and he spied the distant object in midriver. It took shape as he rode, becoming a large raft with the logs atop it stacked in two sections that took up most of the surface. As he drew closer, he saw that the raft had a long tiller at one end. There were only two figures visible, neither Judge Little. He frowned as he drew opposite the raft, but stayed inside the treeline. The two men relaxed at each of the rear corners on the raft and lounged against the stacks of logs. The plan called for Trudy to give him five minutes when they reached the raft to take stock of things, and he let his eyes scan the raft again.

He moved his gaze slowly over the two stacks of logs, paused at the two men, and went on. As his gaze traversed the rear of the raft, he became aware of the length of rope that ran from the tiller back between the two stacks of logs. As he watched, he saw the rope pulled and the tiller turn slightly to the right. Fargo's eyes narrowed. Someone worked the tiller by rope from between the two stacks of logs. Judge Harvey Little, he muttered inwardly as he slowed the Ovaro, reached back to the rifle case, and drew the big Sharps out.

The five minutes were up as he brought the rifle to his shoulder, and Trudy's first shot exploded from inside the trees on the opposite bank. One of the two men half-spun, seemed to do a strange dance, and pitched headlong into the water as the other figure threw himself flat on the raft.

Fargo's eyes focused on the entrance of the space between the two stacks of logs. He saw the third figure rush out, a floppy brimmed hat and loose jacket giving him a scarecrowlike appearance. But from under the brim of the hat, Fargo caught a glimpse of silver-white hair as the man dropped to one knee and peered across the river at the opposite bank.

Trudy came into sight from inside the trees, and Fargo saw both man draw guns and send a hail of bullets flying across the water. Trudy raced in and out of the treeline, drawing their fire as Fargo took aim, pressed the trigger, and the big Sharps fired.

The gunslinger who was on one knee as he fired at Trudy's racing figure seemed to half-leap up, turn a somersault, and land on his back at the very edge of the raft. He twitched and his legs slid from the raft into the water where he hung until he twitched again and the rest of his body slid in.

He disappeared under the water, and Fargo saw the third figure dive back between the two stacks of logs. Fargo rode from the trees and started for the river's edge when he caught the glint of sun on a rifle barrel pushed out from between the logs. He swerved as the shot cut through the air, and raced back into the trees as a second shot just missed him. He halted inside the trees and watched Trudy appear again on the opposite bank, firing as she rode toward the bank. But two shots exploded from the logs at the other side of the raft, and Fargo saw Trudy dive from her horse, hit the ground, and roll furiously until she was back to the treeline.

Fargo whirled the Ovaro and rode out of the trees again, firing this time, but his shots merely sent splinters of log flying into the air. The rifle barrel moved between the logs and he ducked low in the saddle as another pair of shots grazed his hat. He swerved the horse back into the trees again, but he'd given Trudy time to get up and retrieve her horse.

He halted and saw Trudy start out of the trees again on the opposite bank. But she was moving carefully this time, he was relieved to see. Two more shots from the raft instantly slammed into the birches inches from where she nosed the horse out, and she backtracked at once to disappear from sight.

Fargo cursed silently. The plan had been at least partly successful. Drawing fire to one another had let them take out the two gunslingers, but he hadn't expected the ease with which the judge had turned the advantage to himself. He had more than one rifle poked through the two stacks of logs and no doubt plenty of handguns. Firing at him from the shore would only result in more showers of log splinters. The judge would remain his one-man fortress, continue to handle the tiller with the rope, and sail until night offered him escape.

There was only one way at the man and that was to get close enough to the raft to take aim between the logs. That meant lining up directly in front of the raft. Fargo slapped the Ovaro's rump and the horse went into a fast canter through the trees. It was damn unlikely the judge would do anything but keep sailing, but if he did, Trudy would be watching from the opposite bank.

Fargo raced on down river. He was out of sight of the raft when he drew to a halt, dismounted, and tethered the horse inside the trees. He shed everything but trousers and gun belt, ran into the water, and plunged in just as the raft came into sight again. The judge continued to sail in the center of the river, as serenely as if nothing at all had happened. As Fargo began to swim toward the raft, he felt the pull of the current growing stronger. He glanced behind him and saw the reason why as a half-dozen rocks jutted from the water along both banks to narrow the river and increase the current that funneled through.

Fargo swam a half-dozen yards upriver, letting the raft come closer. He saw the judge facing the stern of the raft, playing the tiller. He wore two six-guns at his waist, and the rifle in each stack of logs waited to be fired at a second's notice. As the raft moved directly at him, Fargo's lips drew back in a grimace. Silence was the key to it all, and silence was just about impossible. The judge would hear the slightest sound and whirl firing, and there was no way to surface without some sound. No way and yet no other way, Fargo swore as he drew in a deep breath and let himself submerge. He stayed in place, treading water, as the underside of the raft moved closer.

It was almost directly over him when he surfaced, his head breaking clear with the front edge of the raft only inches away. He started to draw his Colt when he saw Judge Little whirl on one knee, gun in hand, firing down the narrow space between the logs. Fargo gulped in air and submerged as the shots hurtled over the top of his head. He saw the bottom of the raft pass over him as he cursed inwardly. It hadn't worked, and now the judge knew he was in the water. The advantage of surprise was shattered, and Fargo swam along under the raft in a race between thought and breath. If the judge stayed between the logs, he was just about untouchable. He had to be made to come out where he could be reached. Fargo felt the last of his breath disappear with the thought, and he let the raft pass over him and surfaced just behind it.

A hail of bullets exploded almost at once as his head came above water at the rear of the raft, and he dived under the surface again. But he had seen something. He struck out underwater with powerful strokes, came up to the rear edge of the raft, and wrapped his arms around the tiller. He yanked and felt it turn as he pulled it hard to the right. He jammed it tight against the edge of the raft, brought his head above water to take in another gasp of air.

"Son of a bitch," he heard Judge Little curse, and the raft resounded with his racing footsteps. Fargo submerged but kept his hold on the bottom half of the tiller as he felt the judge seize the top of the pole and try to free it. Fargo, his arms wrapped tight around the tiller, kept it immobile, and he felt the judge let go. His breath vanishing, Fargo surfaced just as he glimpsed the judge's tall, lean figure bending over the edge of the raft. He glimpsed the stock of the rifle hurtling down at him, and he twisted aside as the weapon smashed into the water. Again, the rifle stock smashed down as the judge tried to bash him atop the head with it. He came closer as Fargo felt the blow strike his shoulder.

He gulped in air and went underwater again, keeping his arms wrapped around the tiller. He saw the shadowy outline of the judge through the water as he continued to ram the rifle stock into the water alongside the tiller. The judge leaned farther over the edge of the raft to drive the rifle down and in under the edge of the logs. Fargo felt the rifle stock miss his head by less than an inch, but the judge pulled back, tried to wrest the tiller free again.

Fargo clung as his breath gave out. He struck out for the surface, came up just as the judge drove the rifle stock downward again. Fargo took the full force of the blow on his forearm, and the sharp pain shot all the way to his shoulder. He held his place as the judge brought the rifle down again, twisted away in the water at the last second, and the heavy stock just grazed his temple.

As the judge started to pull back for another blow, Fargo swung a hand up, curled fingers around the rifle, and yanked. The judge, leaning far out from the raft to strike downward at an angle, lost his precarious balance and flew into the river. As the splash resounded, Fargo caught the edge of the raft and began to pull himself up out of the water. He glanced back and saw the judge had managed to grab hold of the other corner of the raft, and he clambered aboard with the fury of the desperate.

Fargo pushed himself to his feet as the judge went into a half-crouch, measured distances, and tried a running dive for the space between the logs. Fargo met him as he reached it, swung out with a long, looping left just as Judge Little ducked down. The blow caught him on the forehead, enough power in it to send him crashing against the stack of logs. The judge fell, lost the floppy-brimmed hat, and his silver-white hair cascaded out.

Fargo flicked a glance at the far bank of the river and saw Trudy, the rifle at her shoulder, looking for a chance for a clear shot. But the judge was shielded by the stack of logs again as he pushed himself to his feet, and Fargo saw the man glance over at the rifle pushed into the log pile.

"Don't even think about it," Fargo warned. "It's over. Court's adjourned. Forever." He drew the Colt to add the final emphasis to his words.

Judge Little's lean, handsome face grew disdainful. "Get smart for a change, Fargo. I'll give you half the money. It'll be more than you'll make in a lifetime," he said.

"Can't," Fargo said.

"Why not?" Judge Little frowned.

"Too much money all at once gives me indigestion," Fargo said, and the judge's frown turned into a snarl.

"Stupid fool," the judge flung back.

"Hands on your head," Fargo ordered. "Out here," he added, and took a step backward. He had just motioned with the Colt when he felt his feet go out from under him. At the same instant he heard the crash of wood being splintered and smashed. He landed on the floor of the raft on his back, the sound of logs breaking off like toothpicks in his ears. The realization of what had happened trumbled over him.

The tiller he had jammed to one side had stayed

that way and sent the raft crashing into the rocks. He started to push himself to his feet and glimpsed Judge Little trying to climb over the first stack of logs, which were starting to come apart and slide into the river. The man frantically clawed at the heavy logs as they began to roll sideways as the raft, splintered and coming apart, started to sink.

"The money. Goddammit, the money," Judge Little gasped. He clawed his way up onto the logs and fell as they rolled out from under him. Fargo heard the sudden noise to his right, a loud, cracking sound, and he saw the other stack of logs begin to come part. They seemed to roll with a strange slowness at first that took only seconds to change into a crushing mass of wood.

"Look out," he shouted as he flung himself sideways into the water, went under, and came up a second later to see the other stack of logs crashing into the first, pinning the judge under their rolling, crushing weight. He heard the judge's scream, cut off abruptly when a half-dozen rolling, sliding logs swept over him as they rolled across the sinking raft. He caught a last flash of silver-white hair before a log smashed over it, and he pushed himself back through the water, his eyes still on the logs that jammed against the rocks and then began to drift on downriver.

He waited, watched as the logs drifted slowly downriver, followed by pieces of broken, smashed raft. It was all only flotsam now, driftwood aimlessly floating on. Fitting, Fargo thought grimly. A crooked judge didn't deserve anything better than drifwood as a tombstone.

He turned, swam to the shore, and retrieved the Ovaro from the trees. When he crossed the river,

Trudy sat waiting at the shore, her gaze fixed downriver where the last log had gone out of sight.

"Thief River," she murmured. "He wasn't the first. It's earned its name, I'm sure."

"And he won't be the last," Fargo said. "Let's ride."

Trudy rode back to town with him, and he could feel the mixture of elation and distaste that ran inside her. Emotions that pretty much mirrored his own. Something about a crooked judge always left an especially sour taste in his mouth.

Sheriff Covey's reactions were exactly as Fargo had predicted: caution, checking out their story, and finally a bitter admission, a good man who had to face the truth of having been taken in by those he respected.

It was later, her brother freed and cleared of all charges, that Trudy found him as he just finished currying the Ovaro. "Going someplace?" she asked.

"Someplace," he said. "Don't know where yet."

"We'd make a great team, Fargo," she said.

He smiled at her as he thought for a moment. "Maybe someday," he said finally.

"When?" she thrust at him.

"When I get tired and you get smarter," he said.

"Go to hell," Trudy glowered.

"Where's Jack?" he asked her.

"Headed back home. He told me how he was going. I'll catch up with him," she said. She peered hard at him, a tiny furrow touching her brow. "You're going to visit Alva, aren't you? Finish what you never did the other night with the judge waiting outside."

"Hadn't entered my mind," Fargo said. "Hadn't you best start catching up to Jack?"

She pushed against him, kissed him quickly, and swung onto the bay mare to ride away without glancing back. He watched her go, a smile touching his lips, and he finished currying the horse, put his gear away, and swung into the saddle.

He turned the pinto south, rode into the stand of thick birches, and sent the horse into a fast canter. Alva's place lay directly south, beyond the forest and across the low hill. He hurried the horse, turned into a particularly dense thicket of birch, and raised his arms as he rode beneath a tree that leaned over the pathway. He seized a low branch as he rode under it, pulled up out of the saddle, and brought his legs up to straddle the branch. He hung there and waited, only a few moments passing before Trudy rode up, moving fast under the branch, her eyes on the ground.

He dropped just as she passed under him, came down just in back of her, and yanked her from the saddle. He landed in a thicket of brush with her, and she sputtered, whirled on him with her pert face full of fury.

"Surprise," he said. "Second time around. You've a lot to learn yet, honey."

"Don't you ever tell the truth?" Trudy threw at him accusingly.

"Don't you ever believe anybody?" he tossed back.

"You were on your way to Alva's. I was right."

"Wrong. I figured you'd do just what you did," he said. "I told you, being a trailsman takes knowing people as well as trails."

She glowered, her face a pout. "If you know so much, then you ought to know why I'm here," she said.

"I do." He grinned as he pushed her gently back

onto the soft grass. "And I never disappoint a lady, espcially a fellow trailslady." His mouth found hers and her hands sought him at once.

Alva would wait.

LOOKING FORWARD!

**The following is the opening section
from the next novel in the exciting
Trailsman series from Signet:**

**The Trailsman #56
Guns of Hungry Horse**

---

*1860, the northwest corner
of the rugged Montana territory,
at the edge of the Rockies
and just east of Hungry Horse . . .*

The man had the look, the feel, even the smell of death. His chalk-white face had the color of death. He even rode a pale horse. And why not? He was death, the spirit of death made real. His tall, gaunt figure clothed entirely in black, top hat, frock coat, narrow trousers and boots, all black as a raven's wing. The man moved his pale horse with slow, deliberate steps, his gaunt, hollowed face a cadaverous mask. It would soon be time to don his black mask. He was nearing the town, and he never entered a town without his mask in place. From the Rio Grande to the Alberta border he was known, Caul the Masked Hangman, the very best at his trade.

None ever survived the rope of the Masked Hangman, as sometimes happened with other hangmen. If, for some unaccountable reason, the noose failed to do its job, he was always ready with a single shot to the temple. No one ever cheated him. He was the very best because he liked his work. Caul the Masked Hangman smiled sickly as he rode. He liked the smell of death, the sound of the snap of a vertebra, the wheezing, last, half-second gasp for life. But most of all he enjoyed that instant of final realization that flashed in the eyes of the most hard-bitten. He liked being the holder of that final, absolute power from which there was no recourse. He was finality.

The mask was to insure his anonymity, to keep the buzzards who would avenge their friends from bothering him. He didn't fear them. He simply didn't want the annoyance of having to deal with them.

He continued to ride slowly down the narrow roadway. Caul the Masked Hangman looked forward to mounting the gallows that would be ready and waiting for him. He always insisted on everything in readiness. His task was not to wait around. He was an artist, his task to administer that final answer with style and efficiency.

And, of course, there would be a crowd gathered. There always was, their eyes watching his every move, secretly hoping he would fail for in his failure lay the hopes of their own tomorrows.

Only he never failed and that was also why they came to watch, torn between awe and admiration, fear and fascination, hate inside their every hurrah. And why not? For in him they watched the very best—Caul the Masked Hangman, the last word.

The big man sat quietly astride the magnificent

Ovaro, the horse's white midsection gleaming in the sun, the jet-black fore and hind quarters glistening. The man's lake-blue eyes narrowed as they peered down the road at the black-clothed figure that moved toward him on the pale horse. He took in the measure of the gaunt figure that approached, his long arms, long legs, wide shoulders and black clothes that draped loosely on the tall frame. He nodded to himself in satisfaction, waiting motionless as the pale horse drew near.

Skye Fargo's intense, chiseled handsomeness was as if carved in stone, the muscles of his jaw throbbingly tight. He didn't enjoy what he had to do but he had no choice. He grimaced inwardly. It was the only way, and he only hoped it could be done with as little trouble as possible.

The man on the pale horse reined up and Fargo went cold inside as he stared at the eyes that burned with a pale light as cold as death itself. The man spoke, his voice deep, sepulchral.

"You are in my way," he intoned.

"I know." Fargo nodded.

"Do you know whose path you dare to block?" the man asked.

"Yes. You are Caul the Masked Hangman," Fargo said.

"Most men would not dare to stand in my way," the hangman said.

"I'm not most men," Fargo said.

"You are a bigger fool than most," the hangman said.

"Maybe," Fargo agreed.

"I have no time for fools. I must be somewhere

before noon," the man said, irritation rising in his voice.

"And you're never late," Fargo said.

"Never."

"This time will be different," Fargo answered.

A frown dug into the gaunt face. "Different?" the hangman echoed.

"I'm going in your place," Fargo murmured.

The frown became a frigid stare of disbelief.

"You're not a fool. You're some kind of madman," the man said.

Fargo sighed with resignation. "Probably," he agreed. "But I'm still going in your place."

Fargo saw the pale eyes flicker, caught the movement at the right side of the black frock coat and drew his Colt with a motion as fast as a diamondback's strike. The hangman stared at the barrel of the sixgun pointed at his chest and let his hand drop to his side.

"That's smart," Fargo said softly, silently relieved. Gunplay was the last thing he wanted. There'd be enough of that when the time came without adding Caul the Masked Hangman.

"Get off the horse," he ordered and watched the tall, gaunt form swing to the ground, the man's movements somehow scarecrow-like. Fargo slid from the Ovaro.

"Toss your gun down, nice and slow," he said, and his eyes stayed on the man's hand as he drew the gun from inside the frock coat, a Colt Paterson pocket pistol.

The hangman let the gun drop to the ground and took a long step backward. Fargo moved forward, bent down and started to scoop up the gun when he saw the black arm shoot out and downward with astonishing speed. The blow caught him alongside the temple before he could bring the Colt up. He felt himself go down as bright red and yellow flashes exploded in his head. He hit the ground and the flashing lights snapped off just in time for him to see the long, black leg kick out, the blow smashing into his ribs. He went backwards, grimaced at the sharp pain, and the Colt skittered out of his hand as he half-rolled.

He managed to bring his hands up as the cadaverous face loomed over him and big hands closed around his neck. Breath became labored instantly as the hangman closed his long, powerful fingers. Fargo brought his arms up, tried to pry the man's grip away from his throat, and found the gaunt figure was made of boney strength. He pressed outwards with his arms but the hangman's grip stayed around his throat.

His breath becoming little more than a hoarse rasp, Fargo drew his right arm back, drove a straight, short blow with piston-like force into the man's solar-plexus. The hangman grunted, doubled half-over, and his hands around Fargo's throat fell away.

Fargo brought up a short, sharp uppercut that landed flush on the long jaw, and the hangman went down on one knee, shook his head and dived forward to wrap both arms around his foe. Again, Fargo felt the hard-boned strength of a man, the long arms crushing his ribs. Fargo arched himself backwards, brought one arm up and around and crashed his fist against the side of the hangman's jaw. The man grunted, stumbled, dropped to one knee but still hung on with his rib-crushing grip.

Fargo brought one knee up, drove it into the man's

belly, and the long figure came forward with an oath of pain as his arms relaxed their vise-like grip.

Fargo's right came up in a short arc inside the relaxed arms, all the strength of his biceps behind the blow. It caught the man on the point of the jaw and he fell backwards, doubled in two as if he were doing some kind of backbend. He held there for a moment and then collapsed unconscious, and Fargo pushed him onto his side with one foot. Fargo drew a long breath in, waited a moment, and then began to undress the unconscious figure. He took off all the man's black, outer clothing, stepped to the Ovaro and brought his lariat back. He tied the tall, boney figure, wrists behind his back, first, then ankles and a last length of rope pinning his arms to his sides.

He finished, straightened, his mouth a thin line. It was the only way. He'd realized that much when he learned that Sam Tyler was going to be hanged, and Caul the Masked Hangman had been called in to do the job. He had nosed around, probed and found that there was no other way to change the planned event. Too many powerful people seemed anxious to have Sam Tyler hanged. The wheels had been set in motion, everything made ready.

But he had come too long a way to let that happen, Fargo grunted silently. Too long a way with old promises and new commitments inside himself, a two-way parley he had to follow through to the finish. Fargo dragged the still-unconscious figure away from the road and put the hangman into a thick cluster of bottlebrush at the edge of a wide-limbed hackberry. He stared down at the still-unconscious form of Caul the Masked Hangman and grimaced.

The man was more than a hangman, the job more

than a living. He fancied himself as an avenger, and he gloried in his grisly work. His failure to hang Sam Tyler would not only be a personal insult but a disruption of his mission in the world. He'd be consumed with rage when he woke, Fargo knew, for Caul the Masked Hangman was, in his own way, as much a killer as those he delighted in hanging.

Tough shit, pal, Fargo muttered inwardly as he turned away. He estimated it would be at least an hour, maybe two, before the hangman could free himself after he woke. Without a horse it'd take him nearly another two hours to reach Clear Creek. It would all be over by then, one way or the other.

Fargo halted at the pile of black clothing and began to undress. He stowed his own clothes into the saddlebag on the pinto and pulled on the hangman's clothes. They fit, barely. The pants were a little too tight, and boots much too tight. But all in all he managed to don everything. He pulled the black mask from the pocket of the frock coat and put it on. It covered his face from his upper lip to his hairline, and he put the black top hat on last as he swung onto the pale horse. With the Ovaro following, he slowly rode forward along the narrow road.

When the buildings of the town of Clear Creek finally came into sight, he guided the horses under a line of alders and tethered the Ovaro to a low branch. He gazed upward to see the sun was almost into the noon sky.

They would be waiting, he knew, and he urged the pale horse forward in a slow, steady walk. The questions, the misgivings and mixed emotions all tried to flood back over him, but he flung them aside. There'd be time for sorting out, later, when he had done his own questioning.

The town of Clear Creek took shape, nothing about it any different than a hundred other towns. There was the single, wide main street, the center artery of its existence, with the usual collection of small stores and warehouses on both sides. But Clear Creek was more crowded than usual, he was certain. Hangings always drew an extra crowd, and as he entered the town, keeping the pale horse at its slow walk, he saw the stares that followed him as he rode toward the center of town. The hanging scaffold had been erected there, he saw from behind his black mask, the crowd four deep around three sides of the platform that was raised some ten feet from the ground. The long rope with the noose at the end of it swayed gently in a mild breeze atop the platform.

Fargo drew to a halt, and a man detached himself from the others and came forward, a star-shaped badge on a worn shirt. He looked up at the black-clothed figure out of a nervous, twitchy face.

"Sheriff Snyder," he introduced himself. "We're all ready for you."

Fargo nodded. "Hear tell the man still says he shot in a fair fight," Fargo said carefully.

"Don't they all?" the Sheriff answered harshly, and Fargo nodded at the truth of his remark. "He shot Frank Danbury's boy in the back, according to Frank," the sheriff added.

"Did he shoot him in the back?" Fargo asked.

"It was hard to tell," the Sheriff said, and his face twitched. Fargo was glad for the black mask that hid the contempt in his face.

"You mean you didn't look hard," he said.

The Sheriff shrugged. "Frank Danbury carries a lot of weight around here," he muttered, and his eyes narrowed at the big man. "You come here to talk or hang?" he snapped.

"Bring the prisoner out," Fargo said, and his glance scanned the crowd, pausing at a big man wearing a black tie.

There was an air of authority in the face hard and stiff as a pine board. Two hard-eyed men stood at his side and Fargo saw the Sheriff wave his arm. Fargo turned the pale horse, positioned the animal directly under the edge of the platform, opposite the half-dozen wood steps on the other side. He dismounted and climbed the steps to the platform and the dangling noose.

He let himself appear to examine the noose, walking around it carefully, and giving it a small tug. But behind the mask, his eyes swept the crowd below, and he saw the Sheriff and two men with deputy badges push their way through the onlookers. He saw nothing to make him change his plans.

The Sheirff and his men would shoot. So would Frank Danbury and his two men. But not until they'd recovered from their initial surprise. Fargo guessed he'd have maybe thirty seconds before all hell broke loose. Not a hell of a lot of time. Yet enough if everything went right, he muttered inwardly.

His eyes went to the steps where the Sheriff and his deputies brought their prisoner up to the platform, and he kept the tiny grunt of amazement inside himself. The years had hardly changed Sam Tyler. He looked ten years younger than he was, but then he'd always looked that way. His face still held the boyish charm that helped soften the hardness of his eyes.

Sam Tyler had always been something of a smooth con man, always out for himself and to hell with right and wrong. Yet, when least expected, he could toss aside his usual selfishness.

Sam Tyler had always been an enigma, one of those men you could like while you were disliking. Even now he approached the gallows with an insouciance, a swagger that, while perhaps hollow, put on a good show for those watching.

The Sheriff brought Sam Tyler to stand under the noose and stepped back with his two deputies to wait at the edge of the steps. Fargo's eyes swept the scene once more, saw Frank Danbury's pine-board face watching intently, his two hands equally absorbed. Thirty seconds, Fargo reminded himself again. The rest of the crowd would do nothing except get in the way. Not right away, at least. He stepped around behind Sam Tyler and pulled the noose down and placed it around the man's neck.

It was time for a hanging to go wrong.